Forrest Carter whose Indian name is Little Tree, is known as Storyteller in Council to Cherokee Nations : much of the lore passed from generation to generation by word of mouth is found in his stories. Born in the mountain country of east Tennessee and orphaned at the age of five, Carter lived with half-Cherokee grandpa and his full Cherokee grandma until their deaths when he was ten. He has been on his own ever since, working ranches as a cowboy all over the South and the Southwest areas of the United States. Self-educated, Carter has drawn material for his books from his kin, from his Indian friends, and from a diary his great-grandmother kept during the reconstruction period. History is his main interest; he visits libraries wherever he is and has steeped himself in the history of the South-Southwest and the Indian. His Indian friends always share a part of his earnings from his writing.

Also by Forrest Carter

THE OUTLAW JOSEY WALES

Forrest Carter

The Vengeance Trail
of Josey Wales

Futura Publications Limited
A Futura Book

A Futura Book

First published in Great Britain by
Futura Publications Limited in 1977

Copyright © Forrest Carter 1976

ISBN 0 8600 7514 1
Printed in Great Britain by
Hazell Watson & Viney Ltd
Aylesbury, Bucks

Futura Publications Limited
110 Warner Road
Camberwell, London SE5

To the Apache

1

Pablo Gonzales felt the change. That winter morning of 1868, he squatted against the adobe wall of the Lost Lady Saloon and contemplated his bare feet, and waited out the hours until sundown.

At sundown, Santo Rio reeled drunkenly alive, and men came and drank and whored. In their leaving, sometimes they tossed coins to this one-armed peon, who bowed and smiled and swept his straw hat in the dust. Sometimes they kicked him and laughed when he cowered on the ground.

Pablo felt no bitterness. He had been born to peonage, and now useless to grip the hoe or plow, he accepted his position of scavenger without question.

FORREST CARTER

But the sharpened instinct for survival still lived in
Pablo Gonzales—nature's compensation to the unlanded
peon.

And so he first felt the sound, rather than heard. He
raised his eyes, past the Mexican children playing in the
street, past the Majestic Hotel, and followed the rutted
road where it dipped into the Rio Grande and dissipated
aimlessly in the broken wastes of Mexico on the other side.

And now he heard it clearly, the measured tramp of
many horses and the sound of saddles creaking, and the
ominous jingling spurs that always accompanied the
approach of Rurales.

The sun still shone, but the slanting rays turned metallic
and steel-glinted to Pablo Gonzales. So it always shone on
the presence of Rurales.

Pablo Gonzales' nostrils quivered at the musty smell of
death. A woman's short laugh burst from the saloon. Pablo
did not hear. He had vanished.

He did not seek the 'dobe hovels, but ran for open country with its mesquite and cholla brush. In his passing, he
whistled a soft warning, and the children, old-cunning
through their station of birth, disappeared. A dog tucked
his tail, whimpering to his hiding.

The Texas border town of Santo Rio lay unsuspecting
in its morning stupor as it received Capitan Jesus Escobedo
and half a hundred of his Rurales.

Hard-drinking vaqueros had made a long night for
Kelly, the bartender of the Lost Lady Saloon. He moved in
sour silence, mopping the stinking puddles from tables,
straightening the overturned chairs.

It was Rose, the lady-in-waiting, who had laughed,
warmed by the first drink of the day and remembering the
free-spending vaqueros.

The Rurales were hitching their horses when Kelly saw

them. The color drained from his face and left the pock-marks shadowing his whiteness.

"Rurales!" he whispered hoarsely. He turned to Rose at the bar. "Rurales!" he repeated dumbly.

Now they could hear them, shouting and laughing, flinging themselves from their horses in the peculiar wild abandon that marked their habits.

"God! Oh God!" Rose breathed.

Kelly stared stupidly at her. "Where's Ten Spot?"

"He's at the hotel," Rose whispered.

"Git," Kelly's whisper was hoarse, "git to the back room. Stay hid, tell Melina to stay hid. God's sake, stay hid."

Rose was already running on tiptoe, and closed the heavy door of the back room behind her.

They came jostling through the batwing doors of the Lost Lady, and their laughter died as they entered. Kelly placed himself behind the bar and smiled, a sickly slash of strained lips.

Still they came, circling to stand against the walls. Now they tore the batwings from the doorway and laughed with childish hysteria as they flung them across the saloon.

Some wore sombreros low, to the eyes; others pushed them back, dangling on cords behind hairy necks. They smiled fixedly at Kelly, as with a private joke they intended soon to reveal; brutish smiles, fanging teeth beneath drooping mustaches, matted beards.

Their short jackets and flared chaparrals were filthy with trail dust. Kelly felt a leap of horror at the dried blood on their clothing. Huge pistolas were shoved into belts; long knives hung on their hips, and on some, about their necks. They brought their rifles into the saloon with them.

Two rows deep, they stood around the wall and crowded to the bar. Then they parted for their Capitan.

His appearance brought a sudden rush of warmth to

Kelly, as one locked in a room with insane people might feel upon seeing a calm administrator of authority come to set matters right.

Capitan Jesus Escobedo wore the official army cap, which in itself spoke of order. He was cleanly shaved, with a thin mustache and stylish sideburns, and wore a saber buckled around a trim waist.

"Buenos dias, señor," he smiled politely over the bar at Kelly and extended his hand. Kelly grabbed it with enthusiasm.

"Bane-us dee-ass," Kelly fairly shouted, and felt only the slightest doubt at the glitter of the Capitan's eyes. But then Kelly did not know Captain Jesus Escobedo. The doubt grew uncomfortably with the ripple of giggles that circled the room.

Capitan Jesus Escobedo was an educated man. Beyond that, he was quite certain that his lineage was blooded with royal aristocracy. Perhaps that is why he had sided with Maximilian, the comic-tragic "Emperor of Mexico" appointed by Napoleon III.

Capitan Escobedo had served under the incredibly cruel Colonel François Achille Dupin, who relished warfare on the helpless and devised methods to satisfy his appetite.

"When you kill a Mexican, that is the end of him," Dupin had instructed his officers, "but when you cut off an arm or a leg, or blind his eyes with the hot iron, then he is thrown upon the charity of his friends. This requires more Mexicans to feed him. Those who raise corn cannot make soldiers. Maim or blind all prisoners." And so they did, leaving a monument of living carnage throughout all of northern Mexico.

Only last year, Maximilian had stupidly stood before the firing squad on El Cerro de las Campanas, The Hill of the Bells, and ended the dream of Napoleon the Little; but not that of Capitan Jesus Escobedo.

His uncle, General Mariano Escobedo, had served the Indian, Benito Juarez, and had in fact accepted the surrender of the foolish Austrian. And so Capitan Jesus Escobedo's promotion required a mere shrug of the shoulders: he was appointed to command a district; after all, aristocracy must take care of its own. What the little Indian in faraway Ciudad de Mexico did not know, of course, would cause him no ill.

In truth, Capitan Escobedo hated Benito Juarez, as he hated all Indians. He despised all peons and saw unthinkable chaos as a result of Juarez' announced plan to give land to them.

Through his service to Dupin, a slumbering sadism was awakened as he practiced the crippling art on screaming victims. It grew sharp-edged, as he became more imaginative. Capitan Jesus Escobedo was insane, but with a cunning and a polish of exquisite sadism that made him lend rationality to his acts, as it is with all such men of authority.

His half-wild Rurales riders were his absolute power over the district, and to control such power—he shrugged at the thought—it was necessary to "loosen the leashes . . . on occasion."

Now he pulled a handkerchief from his pocket and delicately dabbed at his forehead. Kelly watched him hungrily.

"My soldados," he said, "have ridden far, señor. Perhaps . . . ," he paused and looked around the room, "perhaps a drink for each of them before we resume our journey?" He smiled quickly with brilliant teeth. "We shall pay—in gold, of course."

"Why shore—shore!" Kelly said heartily, and set bottles of Red Dog on the bar. Eager hands passed the bottles to others around the room. Kelly turned and placed more bottles, and then hesitantly, still more. The hands reached for more. Kelly looked at the Capitan. He was still smiling.

"I am afraid, señor," he purred softly, "my riders are so like the niños, the children. They will require your benevolence. Por favor!"

Kelly emptied his shelves, but now his hands shook. He watched the brute faces upturning the raw liquor, and he shuddered while his mind raced ahead. Kelly had been in tight places before. The Capitan was pouring himself a drink.

"Well! Well!" Kelly exclaimed with false humor, "your boys drink like the U.S. Cavalry patrol boys that come by. They'll be glad to hear you boys paid a visit to the U.S.A." Kelly emphasized "U.S.A."

The Capitan raised an eyebrow as he poured another drink. His face furrowed in puzzlement. "Cavalry patrol?" he questioned politely. "But, mi amigo, you have no cavalry patrol on the border, and . . . ," a recovering smile broke his face, "in truth, Texas is not in the United States —so we have been officially informed. You are—is it not the Confederacy?" he asked politely.

"Oh no," Kelly laughed. "Ain't you heard? The war is over. Texas is back in the U.S.A. all right—yessir, the U.S.A."

The Capitan downed his drink and poured another. A chair crashed in the saloon and there was loud cursing. "Hola!" a Rurale shouted, "Musica!"

A rider leaped on a table and strummed a guitar. Booted feet stomped the floor and a bottle shattered against the wall. The Capitan seemed not to hear any of it. Mock doubt crossed his face as he looked at Kelly, "It's unthinkable, señor. No, I will not believe you, you are making the joke, señor." His tongue was thickening, and he wagged his head in remorse. "To make light of poor soldados who have been fighting the Apache . . ." The Capitan shook his head sadly.

"No!" Kelly said earnestly. He raised his voice to be heard above the growing noise, "No, really . . ."

Loud arguing and cursing rose above the din. Capitan Escobedo watched a bearded Rurale break a bottle in the face of another, sprawling him on the floor. There was uproarious laughter.

He turned to Kelly, "You comprendes, señor? My men are fretful, disappointed. The Apache camp had only the bitches, the women—and the bastardos, niños, the children. The bucks were not there. And while my superiors pay a hundred pesos for the scalp of the Apache buck, they pay only fifty for the bitch, twenty-five for the bastardos." The Capitan pointed toward the milling, stomping Rurales. "See, señor, the picayune hair at their belts; it is enough to disappoint the best soldado."

He leaned into Kelly's face and his eyes glittered with slyness. "Perhaps you have entertainment about, señor, for the temperamento of my poor soldados?"

Kelly was not a brave man. He saw the black hair bundles that dangled from the belts of the Rurales, the dark clots of bloodied ends where the scalp had been cut from the skull. They were from small heads—children's heads.

Kelly felt the strength drain downward, making his legs watery and uncontrollable. He knew quite suddenly that the Capitan was playing with him, and shortly would require more, much more amusement than the mere sight of Kelly withering in fear. If someone else could be the center of attention—not himself! Wildly, his mind raced; after all they *were* whores, Rose and Melina. His eyes sought the door to the back room.

The Capitan caught the movement of Kelly's eyes. "Ah!

amigo, you are a man of compassion." He clapped his hands and shouted, pointing to the door in the rear.

Kelly was overcome by his sin. He snatched bottles from beneath the bar and pushed them at the Capitan, "SEE!" he shouted, and stooped, coming up with more bottles, "SEE! LOOK!" He directed his shout toward the dozen Rurales rushing for the door. No one noticed him. They were almost to the door, when slowly, it opened.

It was Rose. She had dressed for the occasion, a scarlet dress with little glass sequins sewn on, picking up the light and flashing. It was tight-fitting, accentuating the broad full hips and rounding belly, the heavy breasts that pushed together in a huge snowy crevasse, straining over the low-cut front. It took attention away from the gray streaks in her orange dyed hair and the sag of jowls beneath the heavy make-up.

Silence dropped over the room. Rose calmly closed the door behind her. Her face was unnaturally white, but she smiled teasingly, threw her arms wide and walked on high heels toward the Capitan. Her large breasts bounced with a quivering promise as she walked and her buttocks fought the tight satin. Kelly groaned.

"Well, boys!" she shouted, and giggled, "Since I'm all there is, let's have a little drinkee and make fun."

The roar of the Rurales carried undertones of savage anticipation. Kelly saw a nerve jerk the face of Rose, but the smile stayed and there was no hesitation in her walk to the bar.

The Capitan pushed a bottle toward her. Rose tilted it for a long gulping drink. The Rurales crowded around, almost over her. One reached, and caressed the bareness of her breasts, running his hand down the deep cleavage, and gripping brutally.

"Grande!" he shouted, "grande mucho!" Rose shot a stream of Red Dog into his face. The Rurales roared.

"Un momento . . ." The Capitan looked archly at Rose. "What more might we find beyond your door, señorita?"

Rose raised the bottle again and spat whiskey into the Capitan's brilliant smile. He slapped her hard, bringing blood thinning from a corner of her mouth.

"The door!" he shouted. A mob of Rurales crashed the door.

She could not have been more than sixteen. Mexican-Indian peon, long black hair framing the little oval face and falling over the cheap white dress. She stumbled on high heels, whimpering as the hands pushed and pulled, wrapping in her hair, arching her body backward. A low "Ahhhhhhhhh!" swept the room.

"She jest stopped by!" Rose shouted. The Capitan threw back his head and laughed.

"She's the daughter of a *patrón*!" Rose screamed, but her voice carried no conviction.

"Música!" shouted the Capitan, and tilted his bottle. He was becoming drunk. The Rurales stomped their feet in slow cadence while a guitar picked up a rhythm.

Rose pushed away from the bar, but the Capitan signaled and two grinning Rurales wrapped their arms around her, pinning her between them. Pulling her large breasts from her dress, they laughed, bouncing them with their hands, twisting and squeezing while they watched Melina.

The slender girl made a valiant effort. First one and another grabbed her, jostling her in a wild dance around a circle of Rurales. The stomping thundered louder and faster.

She kept up the desperate dance, her small feet moving rapidly, even after the back of her dress had been torn away, and the front—and she danced entirely naked except for the stockings and the high-heeled dainty shoes.

Her body, small-tipped breasts turning upward, was lithe

and brown. She moved faster as the heavy boots picked up the rhythm. The circle became smaller. Her movements were a physical reflex to the sound. Her eyes were bright and hysterical.

The slender body rippled sensuously, perspiration sleeking the curves. The stomping became unbearable to the ear, and heavy breathing brought the air lustfully alive.

Her knees began to wobble. A huge Rurale snatched her from the grasp of another and jostled her furiously around the circle once, twice, lifting her in the air, gripping her body close, and he slid her down against his hardness. Her knees buckled.

He brought his big bulk down upon her, flattening her on the floor. "Ahhhhhhhh!" rose from the breathing. The circle closed in around them.

He moved his body in, between her legs. Pinning her hands to the floor, he brought his bearded face down and bit her mouth.

She twisted her slender hips left as he nakedly hunted for her. With a quick shove, he almost succeeded, but she twisted her hips to the right. With each movement a shout of "Ole!" went up. Again—and again.

She brought her knees up, placing her weight on her dainty feet and arching her hips in the air. Her eyes showed the desperation of her mistake as she felt him under her. The slender legs began to tremble as she tried to hold herself up; but slowly, slowly, she came down.

Suddenly the big hips of the Rurale plunged. She screamed, high-pitched, piercing the air, and her head flopped up from the floor, then back down, like a wounded animal. She screamed again . . . again; her body worked furiously in a frenzy of pain, twisting . . . up . . . down . . . arching . . . out of control as the Rurale plunged again, more rapidly now.

She was still screaming as he rolled from her and another plunged in his place—and another. The passion heat maddened the waiting Rurales. They argued and fought for position.

Now she lay limp, unconscious. First they twisted her arms to bring back movement to her body; after that, they touched lighted cigarillos to her to produce convulsive twitches at climactic moments . . . until the body would no longer twitch, as they held her in grotesque positions. The smell of burnt flesh hung in the air.

The Capitan watched, fascinated. Beads of sweat pimpled his face. Tears made thick trails in Rose's heavy make-up. She didn't sob. She didn't know she was crying. Kelly closed his eyes and sank to the floor behind the bar.

The flat bang of a small pistol split the closeness of the room, and the Rurales pushed back from one man, who staggered and fell.

Ten Spot stood in the door, a smoking derringer in his hand. He was hatless, neatly dressed in the black coat and ruffled shirt of a gambler. He saw the Capitan and coolly raised the ugly little pistol; but he never shot. A rifle cracked in the hands of a Rurale, knocking Ten Spot backward in a half flip. He spraddled in the doorway, legs jerking, and lay still.

Rose screamed. She lunged, grabbing a bottle and smashing it into the face of the nearest Rurale. Her mouth twisted maniacally. "You goddamned sonofabitches!" she screamed, and rushed at the Capitan, clawing his face.

They fell on her, angry dogs, mad with more than lust. But she fought. They dragged her to the middle of the room and ripped away the shiny satin dress. She screamed no more, but bit and kicked, and punched with her fists— and when her hands were pinned to the floor, she fought them with her feet. There was no laughter.

Her huge legs forced open, she took them, one by one, chewing at her breasts, as her body weakened. They kicked her face, smashed at her body until she lay unconscious. Her flesh no longer quivered.

The Capitan watched it all, intense, lips parted. He had them drag Kelly from behind the bar, and they shoved him down on the body of Rose.

"Perform for us, gringo!" The Capitan spat on him. Kelly cried. Tears rolled down the pouches of his face as he lay on Rose's naked body, his face inches from hers. His body shook with broken sobs.

Rose's left arm lay twisted unnaturally backward, almost pulled from its socket. She opened her eyes and looked into Kelly's. Her face, horribly mottled with blood, lips battered outward, broken teeth, twisted in the effort to speak.

"Rose . . . Rose . . . ," Kelly whispered brokenly, "I'm sorry, Rose . . . please . . . forgive me, Rose," and he buried his head in her breasts.

Rose raised a ponderous right arm and draped it uselessly around Kelly's neck. She whispered, "Pore Kelly . . . you didn't . . . deal it, podner . . . it jest . . . come up . . . busted flush . . ." Her eyes glazed and she sighed.

The Rurales had spent their passion. Now their thinking turned superstitiously on the death around them. A few crossed themselves. They grumbled and shuffled about, looking for whiskey, ready to quit and be gone.

The Capitan placed his boot on the chest of Ten Spot.

"This one breathes," he said. "Throw him over a horse. If he lives he must be executed."

Kelly stood dumbly in their midst and watched as they dragged Ten Spot to the horses.

"And now . . . ," the Capitan turned to face Kelly, once more the precise army officer, "we must see to you, mi amigo." He held his hand palm upward toward a Rurale, who placed a big pistola in his grip. He smiled and casually shot Kelly in the chest.

Kelly stumbled backward and sat down, his back against the bar. Blood spread over his shirt and small red bubbles puffed out from his lips. Then Kelly did a strange thing. He laughed. He laughed deep in his chest and brayed the laughter from his lips, and coughed, spewing a fog of pink mist, and laughed again.

The Capitan was astonished. He bent forward. "La Muerte, The Death—she is funny?"

Kelly shook his head and chuckled. "Naw," he coughed, "it ain't funny." He shook his head again, wobbling back and forth on his limp neck, and giggled at his secret joke. A red flood gushed over his chin. "Naw," he repeated, weaker now. The Capitan bent lower to hear. "But you are funny, my friend. I know . . . you see . . . yore hide is done measured. I ain't nothin', but . . . ," Kelly coughed, "but you . . . I'd ruther be right here where I am . . . than you. Ten Spot and Rose . . . they're friends of Josey Wales . . . JOSEY WALES!"

Kelly raised his eyes to the Capitan's and grinned horribly. "See ye in hell." And then, for once in his life, Kelly rose supremely to the occasion. He spat blood over the boots of the Capitan before he choked.

"Josey Wales?" the Capitan repeated. He watched his Rurales filing out to their mounts. Half a dozen rummaged behind the bar for whiskey. They brought out a box and turned it up on the bar, spilling the contents. It was all papers, and the papers were posters; the posters were all alike, of one man.

Capitan Escobedo looked down at the face staring up at him from the posters and felt the shock of vicious black eyes, glazed with hate, below the brim of a Confederate cavalry hat. A bone-deep bullet scar split the cheek above a black mustache. Beneath the picture he read:

> JOSEY WALES: AGE 32, 5 FEET 9 INCHES, 160 POUNDS. BULLET SCAR HORIZONTAL RIGHT CHEEKBONE. DEEP KNIFE SCAR LEFT CORNER MOUTH.
>
> PREVIOUSLY LISTED WANTED BY U.S. MILITARY AS EX-GUERRILLA LIEUTENANT SERVING WITH CAPTAIN WILLIAM "BLOODY BILL" ANDERSON IN MISSOURI.
>
> WALES REFUSED AMNESTY AFTER THE SURRENDER, 1865. REGARD AS INSURRECTIONIST REBEL, BANK ROBBER, KNOWN KILLER OF AT LEAST 35 MEN.
>
> ARMED AND DANGEROUS. EXTREMELY QUICK AND PROFICIENT WITH PISTOLS. DO NOT ATTEMPT TO DISARM. REPEAT, DO NOT ATTEMPT TO DISARM.
>
> WANTED DEAD. REPEAT, WANTED DEAD. $7500 REWARD.
>
> U.S. ARMY MILITARY DISTRICT: SOUTHWEST, GENERAL PHILIP SHERIDAN, COMMANDING.

The Capitan studied the posters for a long time. His Rurales were mounted, waiting.

The Missouri guerrillas were known to all military men, even in Mexico; the James boys, the Youngers, Bloody Bill Anderson, Josey Wales, Fletcher Taylor, Quantrill; unreal men of ferocious, blood-crazed reputations . . . unreal.

He rolled the posters together and folded them inside his coat, lifted a last drink from the bottle and led his riders, trailing dust, to the Rio Grande.

He shrugged. He could post the papers in the villages he passed on his way south. It would alert the known pistoleros; such a reward was dinero, mucho.

Still, as he crossed the Rio Grande, he could not restrain

the urge to look back over his shoulder. Curiously, the sun shone with a steel glint. The broken land behind him to the north harbored shadows, black and ominous.

Capitan Jesus Escobedo shivered unexpectedly and felt cold.

2

The sun dropped in the west and streaked red ripples on the Rio Grande, blushing the cactus and mesquite, and fading them purple in the shadows. The first coyote yelped, far away. The wind pushed dust whirls spinning down the street of Santo Rio. No one ventured forth.

Inside the Lost Lady, Kelly sat piously dead, hands folded before him. His eyes stared at the twisted form of Melina. Even in death, she had a delicate grace, like a ballerina frozen in blood, head bowed in submission.

Pablo Gonzales came back. Like the dog that returns to where he has once been fed, Pablo came back to the Lost Lady. He hesitated on the threshold of this awesome death place, dropping his straw hat to cross himself. He almost fled.

But he was drawn to tiptoe past Kelly and Melina. To Rose.

Rose had put no price on her kindness to him, carelessly slipping the coins into his hand with a wink—or a curse—to hide the giving. And so Pablo came to stand above her, to beseech Our Lady of Guadalupe to speak in her behalf. He had no other gift.

He had been frightened. He should have warned her, and now he was ashamed. For the second time in her life, Rose, the whore, was asked for forgiveness.

Pablo prayed and looked down through the closing shadows at Rose's face. Her eyes were closed—beefy, beaten slits.

The eyes opened. Pablo stumbled backward, but the eyes burned at him, feverish, hypnotic, holding him. Her face twisted; then clearly, hoarsely, the whisper came. "Been holding out . . . Pablo. C'mere . . . close."

Pablo kneeled by her head. "Señorita . . ."

"Shut up!" she commanded. "Listen . . . I cain't hold . . . much longer. Go to Crooked River Ranch . . . Josey Wales . . . ye hear . . . Josey Wales?"

Pablo nodded, "Si, I hear, Señorita Rose."

Rose swallowed and closed her eyes for such a long time that Pablo thought her dead. The great body heaved. The eyes opened. "You tell Josey Wales . . . Ten Spot is alive . . . Ten Spot carried off by Capitan Jesus Escobedo . . . Escobedo . . . Ten Spot . . . ye hear?" She didn't wait for an answer. "Tell Josey I said . . . give you two hundred gold . . . ye'll git it . . . ye hear?"

"Si, but . . ."

She appeared not to listen. "Le' me hear you swear on some of them saints . . . you'll go . . . hurry up!"

Pablo hesitated. Her eyes fluttered open, fixing fiercely on his own. "Swear, goddammit!"

"Santo Pedro—Santo Juan—I will go," Pablo whispered hastily.

Rose sighed. "Tell Josey . . . ," her eyes closed, "tell Josey . . . I shore done tangled . . . the loop this time." Her big breasts quivered in a spasm that hardened the nipples. The spasm moved down her body in a wave, bunching and releasing her belly, jerking the bloody legs.

Pablo felt for the small wooden cross on the string about his neck and held it before her. Her eyes opened. She gazed at it for a long time. The understanding returned. Puffed lips tried to smile. "Thankee, son . . . but reckin . . . a snort of Red Dog . . . would do me more than likely . . . right smart more good." This time, the eyes did not close.

Pablo saw the life take leave, little flickers that grew weaker as it pulled away from the eyes, and left marbles staring at him. He felt her soul brush past him, hurrying, unleashed by the stubborn will. He heard it complain in the low moan of wind that cornered the building and whipped dust through the door. He ran.

He hid in the mule stables, far back behind the foulness of dung heaps. In the night he heard riders and much talk, but he did not move.

Pablo knew the bond of Rose and Ten Spot, and Josey Wales. He had seen him, big pistolas tied on his legs, the giant red horse.

Squatting beneath the batwing doors of the Lost Lady, he had heard Ten Spot the gambler and Rose the whore swear to the government hunters that they had seen Josey Wales killed in Mexico. They had signed the paper. This lie they gave to Josey Wales, as they gave Pablo the coins— for no reason. It was a great gift.

Bandido! The wise and learned clucked their tongues

and shook their heads in disgust. The stupid, plodding peons and their bandido heroes. Beyond comprehension.

But no national heroes for the peon. National meant government, and government meant the shifting, changing wars of politicians and generals. It was the peon who died. The peon who took his wife and children with him to the battlefields; they had nowhere else to go. The peon who died, or came back to the yoke and lived on short rations to pay for the war.

There were the hacendados, the patróns, who owned the land. But as with all men of wealth and power, they rode the tides unbattered, wiggling fish atop the currents. The hacendado paid his tithe to the victor.

For the soldados who crisscrossed his baronage, there were more fundamental appetites to appease. He offered the peons' women for fandangos. The green, unbudded Indian girls for the soldado who sought pain in others with his lust. The ripening, flowered bodies of older girls with their popping breasts and rounding hips for the connoisseur of pure pleasure. The hacendado kept his land.

There was the Church. But the priests and bishops of the Church bureaucracy ate and drank with the hacendados and the generals—and owned countless miles of land, farmed by the peon as tribute to the Church.

The Church had backed Maximilian against the little Indian, Benito Juarez; and the Church told the peon to expect his reward in heaven.

The peon attended the rituals. He sought the supreme unction at death and the blessing at birth; but he prayed, now, to the Santos, the Saints, not the priests, to intercede for his soul with God.

His strength was deceiving, was the peon's. The land he did not own, but farmed, and so loved it the more. Not with a possessive love, nor love of profit, but for what it was—his life.

And so his strength and stubbornness were the strength and stubbornness of the land. Yielding, but not yielding. Plowed and eroded, whipped by storms, but always there. Persisting by presence.

The peon had proved his courage behind the leadership of Benito Juarez. Sandal-footed, straw-sombreroed, with old musket and machete, he had whipped the Emperor's men, and the French, the ones who stayed behind. In truth, he had defeated the hacendados and the Church bureaucracy; but the wiggling fish remained as they were. Now they besieged the hands of Benito in Ciudad de Mexico and lashed the peon on the land, and in the silver mines. Pablo knew. He had carried a musket for Benito. He had lost his arm beneath the chopping hatchet of Dupin.

And so there was only God and the Santos; the land and the bandido.

The bandido was more reckless than the vaquero, wilder than the Rurales. He raided the hacendado and the government, and was damned by the Church, and so he had no soul. He dueled the wiggling fish, lived briefly and died quickly. And with each bandido's death, it was the stubborn, stoic peon who asked the Santos to intercede and return his soul. In this, the peon persisted, and the Church could not stop or dissuade him.

Pancho Morino, Ernesto "El Diablo" Chavez, Chico "Jungle" Patino, once they had been peons. As had the gringo bandido, Josey Wales.

Josey Wales. Pablo knew his life, as an aficionado of bullfights knows the life of a great toreador. Josey Wales had been a peon, a farmer, in a land called Missouri. Men called "Kansas Redlegs," part of the government no doubt, had killed his woman and his niño, and Josey Wales had joined guerrilleros to fight them.

When the revolution failed, Josey Wales would not surrender, as it is with all great bandidos. He had ridden into Texas with a compadre bandido, Lone Watie, of Cherokee Indian blood.

They had killed many men of government with their fast guns, and had taken women to wife and now ranched in the hidden valley to the northwest.

Pablo heard voices. Dawn had come, gray and pinked in the east. He came from behind the dung heaps, and through the stable door watched men digging graves behind the Majestic Hotel. They were burying Kelly and Melina and Rose. The sight brought back his oath. Pablo crept back to his hiding place. There was no one now to hide from; only the oath.

It was cool in the mule stables, but sweat rolled down his body. How far was it? A hundred miles? There was the Apache, the "Enemy," ever present, never relenting from his ghostly haunting of the plains, his horror. There was the Comanche, who never showed mercy. It was impossible.

Morning passed into afternoon, and Pablo crouched in the stable. Twice he walked to the door and came back. He had sworn to the Santos. At sundown, he stole a mule.

Vaguely he knew the Crooked River Ranch lay to the northwest. He headed the mule, old and shuffling, into the landscape of cactus and ocotillo.

The desert brings darkness as it does death, quickly and without warning. There was no moon, but the stars were brilliant in the black bowl. Pablo picked the brightest star to the right of the sun's setting and watched it between the ears of the mule.

Despite the desert night chill, he finally dozed, rocked by the slow plod. In snatches he came awake: when a wolf howled, close and threatening, answered by another; or when the mule stopped, questioning the insanity of carrying a sleeping peon to nowhere in the night. Each time Pablo kicked the mule and placed the star between its ears.

Light glowed in the east when he came to the arroyo. It was deep and narrow and carried the movement of sluggish water at its bottom. He dismounted and led the mule down. They both drank. Pablo squatted, watching the mule suck at the shallow stream, mostly mud. His head fell on his arm and he slept.

It was not the sun that wakened him. It was the sound of an impatient horse, not moving forth, but stomping at the ground. Before he opened his eyes, he knew he was dead.

They sat spotted ponies on the rim of the arroyo, perhaps a dozen. Hair dangled from reins here and there, with fresh pink skin tops that told of a recent raid. It accounted for the two riderless ponies.

Pablo stared, unblinking, and could not move. Without a word, they brought their horses down into the arroyo and dismounted. White and blue paint hideously distorted their faces, displacing the mouth, the chin, the cheek—but not the eyes. With cruel, naked hate, the eyes watched Pablo.

They wore breechclouts and moccasins, with a single feather in the hair. The hair was not loose like the Apache, but long and braided. Comanche!

They closed a circle tightly around Pablo, jerking the mule's rope roughly from him. A warrior wrapped his hand in Pablo's hair and yanked him to his feet, almost off the ground.

He held the hair aloft: "Bon-do-she!" And with a long knife, he lightly circled Pablo's head in a mock scalping motion. There was low laughter. It was not a happy laugh.

The warrior still held his hair, straining the scalp.

"Hablas español?" Pablo asked weakly.

A lean brave pushed his face close to Pablo's and grinned evilly. "Si—Mexicano?" he hissed.

"Si, señores . . . ," Pablo began. The warrior kicked him

between the legs. Pablo bent double, vomiting on the ground. A rifle butt smashed against his head, and he fell, dazed but not unconscious. His groin was swelling; throbbing darts of pain made him retch again.

The warriors left him. Dragging brush together and snapping sticks, they set a fire. Half of them gathered around the mule, and while two held its head, a third glided in to the mule's neck and circled it smoothly, deeply with his knife. The mule thrashed and kicked, but they twisted him to the ground.

While his legs still jerked, their knives moved down the backbone, pulling away the hide, as is the way of the Comanche. Skillfully they butchered and hung the meat, thonged with rawhide, on the back of a horse.

The liver and kidneys they sliced and roasted over the fire. Eating, squatting on their haunches, they paid no attention to Pablo. As they finished, licking the grease from their hands and the mule blood from their arms, their talk was low-toned. The talk was Comanche. Pablo could not understand them.

The sun tilted into the arroyo and lifted the stench of mule offal on the air. Pablo watched first one—three—now ten vultures, wheeling high with the languid patience of scavengers. He would soon join the offal.

Two warriors came; seizing him by the ankles, they dragged him to the fire. Moccasined feet pressed his shoulders to the ground, and they looked down at him while they jerked his pants down around his knees. Pablo watched a tall warrior slowly turning a knife blade over the flames. The horror struck him.

"Estuprador!" a warrior shouted down at him, and spat in his face.

"NO! no rapist, no estuprador!" Pablo shouted. "No. No, señores . . ."

The tall warrior stood over him now, the knife blade

red with heat. His face twisted evilly as he bent, kneeling between Pablo's legs. The faces looked down at him, waiting for the screams, the fear, the pain.

Pablo stopped struggling. He prayed aloud, surprisingly clear in the still air of the arroyo, "Santo Pedro, Santo Juan, take me quickly. I have tried—my oath—to reach Señor Josey Wales. It is not to be." Tears filled his eyes, blurring the warriors, who seemed to stand frozen, statue-like. Pablo waited. Nothing happened. No pain. The Santos had taken away the pain.

His eyes cleared. The warrior with the knife was bending curiously over him "Joh-seh Wales?" the tall warrior asked. Pablo was bewildered.

"Si," he said, "Josey Wales."

The feet were removed from his shoulders. "Joh-seh Wales!" the name was breathed by the warriors.

Excitement, hysteria seized Pablo. He leaped to his feet, pants falling to the ground. "Joh-seh Wales!" he shouted, leaping up and down, genitals flapping. "Joh-seh Wales!"

The warriors took up the shouting, jumping, grabbing Pablo and shaking him. "Joh-seh Wales!"

Pablo beat his breast with his fist and waved his hand in all directions. "Mi amigo! Joh-seh Wales! Vaya! Vamos Joh-seh Wales!" He snatched his pants from the ground, pulling them about his waist, and danced in a circle, wild-eyed.

The warriors lifted him on their shoulders and flung him on a pony. They leaped to their horses, and leading Pablo's among them, set off in a canter to the northwest.

The wind whipped Pablo's hair behind him. He was filled with exhilaration. A miracle! The Santos had wrought a miracle! He felt a destiny! A fate! A mission of the Santos! He was ordained.

Through noon heat and into the afternoon, the tireless Indian ponies cantered and trotted as the Comanche paced them, never stopping. They said nothing, keeping their eyes intently on the horizons around them.

The ground became broken. Jagged buttes rose against the skyline. The sun dropped in the west and died behind a naked mountain far away.

Suddenly the Comanche brought the ponies to a halt. They pulled Pablo's pony up beside the leading warrior. He placed the reins in Pablo's hand and pointed toward the mountain.

"Joh-seh Wales!" he announced, and whipped the rump of Pablo's pony viciously with a leather thong. The pony leaped into a dead run, almost unseating him.

Pablo fought the reins. After a long time he settled the pony into a bone-jarring trot. He looked around him for the Comanche. They were distant, to the south, loping their ponies. They did not look back.

3

A deeper blackness than the sky, the mountain seemed to
recede, and then began to grow: towering, naked with
the broken teeth of butte rock, and then becoming two
mountains, paralleling each other, sloping into the desert.

It was dawn when Pablo turned the slope of the nearest
ridge. A clear creek ran down the valley between the
mountains. At the entrance there was much sign of the
Comanche, and as he walked the pony up the valley, the
brand on trees carried the sign, the brand of the Crooked
River Ranch—but also the wiggling snake sign of the
Comanche.

The grass was knee-deep to the pony, and always the
shallow clear creek ran in the center. There was cotton-

wood and live oak lining the banks of the creek. Pablo saw antelope, black-tail deer, quail and ruff grouse. The sweet virile smell of water, grass, trees, of life, set down between the mountains, shocked the senses of a rider coming from the desert.

Huge dim shapes of longhorn cattle lifted their magnificent heads at his coming, trotting warily away with warning snorts. The valley looked untouched, except for the crooked sign.

Pablo rode on, and the walls lifted higher on either side, coming almost together at places, making a narrow grass-floored arroyo, then opening out a half mile across. Now the light lifted the grayness of early dawn.

Instinctively Pablo looked behind him. A rider followed. He wore a Mexican sombrero and was short-jacketed, with the flared chaparrals of the vaquero. Pablo was afraid to speak or stop. He waved his hand, but the vaquero made no motion that he saw him. Pablo kicked his pony into a trot and heard the horse keep pace behind him.

Steadily he trotted the pony—an hour—two—between the winding sheer walls of the mountains. The longhorns and game were more plentiful, and as he twisted on the pony, looking about him, he saw the vaquero silently keeping pace.

Ahead, the mountains closed together to end the valley. Pablo saw the low adobe ranch house, set back in cottonwood and cedar. Around it were smaller adobes, and behind, a clear waterfall poured from a narrow cleft.

He was almost into the yard of the house when a loud whistle, "SKEEEEeeeeee!" came from the vaquero behind. It was the call of a Tennessee mountain nighthawk, and was instantly answered by a peculiar whipping whistle, the call of a whippoorwill. Both sounds were unfamiliar to Pablo.

But the figure was familiar, stepping casually before

him, blocking his way. Tall; a buckskin shirt hung loosely on the gaunt frame, encircled by a belt holding a sagging pistol. His copper face was bony and wrinkled, framed by braided hair that hung like black whips over his shoulders. He moved in boot moccasins, with a lithe grace that belied his age. Pablo had seen him once in Santo Rio. It was Lone Watie.

Holding the rein of Pablo's pony, he stared up at him, black eyes beneath a gray cavalry hat of the Confederacy.

"Howdy," he said easily.

"Buenos dias, señor, Pablo answered, "I . . ."

"Hold on." Lone raised a hand. "If'n ye're a-goin' to talk Mex, talk to Chato here." He jerked a thumb at the vaquero, who had pulled up beside Pablo.

"No, señor," Pablo said hastily, "I speak inglés. I have come of urgent need to see Señor Josey Wales."

Lone Watie's eyes narrowed to black slits, and the vaquero moved his horse closer to Pablo.

"Josey Wales is dead," Lone said flatly.

"I know . . ." Pablo was uneasy. "That is, I know of Señor Ten Spot, or Señorita Rose. It is from Señorita Rose that I come."

A slow minute ticked away as Lone studied Pablo's face. Morning brush wrens twittered in a tree, and far off a cow bellowed for her calf. Pablo felt his scalp tighten.

Chato leaned from his saddle beside Pablo and placed a hand on his shoulder. "You comprende, señor . . . ," his voice was soft, "if you was to see Josey Wales, you would die, mi amigo, unless acepcion by him—it is a necesidad." White teeth flashed a wicked smile.

"I—must see him," Pablo answered stubbornly. Chato Olivares shrugged his shoulders and looked at Lone. The Cherokee turned without a word and led Pablo's pony to a hitch rail at the rear of the house. They went through the kitchen door, Lone leading, and Chato, spurs jingling, walking behind.

Pablo did not know what he would find beyond the door, but he was unprepared for what he saw.

A long table extended down the room; on it were platters of beef, sides of bacon, plates of beans and biscuits. The heavy smell of cooked food made juices in his mouth.

On one side of the table, a pretty Indian woman was eating, suckling an Indian baby at her shapely breast. Past her, a weathered Anglo cowboy was eating with head-down intentness. Across the table from them, a young blond woman, heavy-breasted, held an equally blond baby on her lap, and next to her, a Mexican vaquero was attacking a plate piled high with food.

At the far end of the table, Pablo saw him, and instinctively crossed himself for the bandido without a soul— Josey Wales!

He looked up at their entrance, black-haired and mustached, a brutal scar jagging his cheekbone. His eyes caught Pablo's, black as the Cherokee's, as hard, capable of cruel light. An old lady, tiny and white-haired, was placing more food on the table.

Lone and Chato tossed their hats on the floor and took seats at the table, Lone next to the Indian woman. She stopped eating and ran her arm around his waist, kissing him on the cheek.

Pablo stood, half bowed, and shuffled uncertainly. Chato, hugely filling his plate, did not look up, but tossed a thumb in Pablo's direction. "This is . . ."

"Pablo Gonzales, señoras and señores," Pablo said politely.

". . . say he has to see you, Josey," Chato finished, and continued with his plate filling.

Josey Wales' hard eyes turned on Pablo. "Well?"

Before Pablo could answer, the old woman pointed to a place at the table and looked at Pablo. "Rat cheer," she said. Pablo looked nervously at the spot she had indicated, but saw no rats.

The blond woman smiled kindly at him. "She means for ye to sit right here," she said, and indicated the place.

"That's what I said," the old lady spoke indignantly.

"Señor?" Pablo asked, looking at Josey Wales.

"Set DOWN!" the old lady said loudly. Pablo sat.

Chato handed him plates of beans, biscuits and meat without looking up from his eating.

Their entrance had apparently interrupted a speech by the white-haired lady, for she began talking in mid-sentence, ". . . an' if'n we don't take some kind of damn mind about hit, Lord knows what this chere place is comin' to. Little Moonlight . . . ," she pointed a finger dramatically at the Indian woman, who was cutting meat from a platter with a wicked-looking knife, "has got ye all half the time tryin' to talk Cheyenne, 'cause *she* ain't got brains enough to learn how to talk. Well, I ain't a-goin' to talk *hit*! An' another thing—air ye listenin', Josey?"

Pablo stole a look at the outlaw. He was chewing tough beef while he ran a hand over the blond baby's head.

"Yes ma'am, Granma," he said without looking up, "I'm listening."

Everyone continued eating. Chato held up an empty platter and Granma took it, refilled it, and set it back on the table. She talked as she brought the food. "An' another thing—HEATHERNISM! Little Moonlight is continual a-hunchin' an' a-pumpin' up on Lone, ever'time the notion strikes her, *rat* out in the open. An' Lone, who was raised to know better, goes at hit with her like a damn boar coon—ye *hear* me, Lone?"

"Yes ma'am, Granma," Lone said humbly. He speared

two biscuits from a passing plate and ladled gravy over them.

"By God," Granma said, putting a plate of bacon beside Pablo's plate, "I don't know what would happen to the raisin' of these two pore young uns ifn hit wa'ant fer me." Suddenly she jabbed Pablo on the shoulder. "Air *you* saved, son?"

Pablo looked bewildered. "Religion," Chato mumbled at him around a mouthful of food.

"Oh, si, señora. I have been christened, I . . ."

"Ye see!" Granma said, "an' *he* ain't got but one arm!" Granma sniffed, looked closely at Pablo, and sniffed again. "But I'll tell ye, son, soon's ye finish eatin', I'll give ye some soft soap. Ye can git in the creek—damned if'n ye don't stink like a hawg—no offense meant, atall."

"Si, I will, señora," Pablo said. "I was held by Comanche and . . ." Everyone looked up from their eating.

Pablo told of the Comanche, how they captured him and butchered his mule, what they did when he used the name of Josey Wales.

"Josey met Ten Bears, a war chief," Granma said quietly, "in the valley. Told him sich as they both could die er live. That we wouldn't dis-spoil the land—they could use hit—we could use hit. When they come through, they make medicine, eat some o' the beef, there in the valley. Hit's a treaty of word, bein' bond. That's the reason they turned ye loose, son. Josey Wales abides his word. Don't ye fergit hit."

"Yes, si, señora, I will not forget," Pablo said, "I . . ." He was going to tell of Señorita Rose, but Granma interrupted, continuing her recitation of the decaying morality about her.

She looked meaningfully at Josey, who was sopping gravy with a biscuit. "Chato there," she pointed at the vaquero, "has total backslid. He might near cusses wuss than Lone. Ye hear me, Chato?"

"Yes ma'am, Granma," Chato mumbled as he chased his food with scalding coffee.

She didn't wait for his acknowledgment. "Travis there, and Miguel has took up tobaccer chewin' and spittin' ever'whares, which they taken from *you*, Josey. An' *yestiddy*," she pointed triumphantly at Little Moonlight, "*yestiddy* I seen *her* chewin' an' a-spittin'. By God, hit's got so a body has to leap like a grasshopper roundst here to keep from gittin' spit on!"

She bent, looking closely at the baby held by the blond woman. "Laura Lee, that young un looks plumb peak-ed. I told ye to give hit a spoon of calum root. C'mere, Jamie." She lifted the baby from Laura Lee's arms.

"Señorita Rose . . . she is dead," Pablo said in the silence. Granma froze, holding the baby in midair. Knives dropped on the table. Every head turned on Pablo.

"My God!" Granma breathed.

4

Pablo told his story. He hesitated at the description of
Rose and Melina. "Tell it all." The steel-soft voice was
Josey Wales'. Pablo told it all. No one spoke when he
finished.

The Indian baby whimpered in the silence, pulled from
its tit and instinctively held tighter by Little Moonlight.

The stillness waited on Josey Wales, for the heat, the
black rage, to fade, to die in his eyes. Slowly came the
sane light of calm deliberation. It was almost physical.
Granma sighed, "Damn!"

Josey motioned to Pablo. "Miguel, take him to the creek
and git him some clothes." Miguel rose silently and
ushered Pablo from the room. The men stood, pushing

back their chairs in unison with Josey Wales. They followed him into the yard.

Beneath the cottonwoods, they sat on heels in a tight circle, shoulders hunched against the wind whining in the canyon: Chato Olivares, Lone Watie, Travis Cobb, and Josey Wales.

With a stick, Chato traced the map of Mexico on the ground. "We are here." He pricked the soil. "Below us, across Rio Grande, is the state of Chihuahua; to the west, Sonora; to the south, Durango. Capitan Escobedo would be of Chihuahua. It is a place—grande, Josey."

Josey Wales slid a long knife from the cavalry boot, cut a plug of tabacco and shoved it into his cheek. He chewed slowly and did not speak.

"Cain't figger it," Travis Cobb drawled, "blottin' ol' Kelly's brand and saddlin' Ten Spot—why not Ten Spot?"

Chato's smile glittered beneath the mustache. "Comprende Capitan Escobedo. He makes a little sport across the border; only putas, whores. He kills the witness, carries back a criminal who, he says, he was chasing. It justifies, if there are questions. Also, Ten Spot will make sport for the Rurales—example to scare the peons. Capitan Escobedo is not only a soldado, he is a politico. Esta uno bueno." Chato shrugged at the simplicity of it.

The men stood, watching Miguel return with Pablo. The peon wore chaparral leggings flared over the high-heeled boots of a vaquero, a tight-fitting jacket with one sleeve pinned to his shoulder, a leather sombrero.

Miguel grinned. "Vaya! El vaquero!" There was a trace of condescension in his laughter. Pablo shifted with embarrassment.

Josey Wales fixed him with a contemplative eye, and spat accurately in the map of Chihuahua.

"What do ye do, son, what's yer trade?" he drawled.

Pablo looked up. "I am—a beggar, señor."

"And before ye was a beggar?"

"I carried a rifle for General Benito Juarez, until . . ." He raised the arm stump. "Before—I was a farmer, señor."

A light flickered, and died, in the eyes of Josey Wales. "I was a farmer—oncet," he said. He was far away for a moment, listening to the wind-whine. The men shuffled awkwardly. Suddenly to Pablo, "How much did Rose promise ye to come here?" At Pablo's surprised look, he laughed shortly. "I know Rose."

"Two hundred gold pesos, señor," Pablo said, "but I will not take it."

"Why not?" Josey's tone was harsh.

"Because—I will not take it," Pablo repeated. Josey watched the stubborn set come to Pablo's jaw.

"Then why did ye come?" and his voice was softer. Pablo shifted uneasily. He felt he was on trial. Did the bandido kill all who did not satisfy his questions?

He shrugged his shoulders helplessly. "Because Señorita Rose was—kind to me." Expecting laughter, he glanced furtively at the men. There was none.

"What ye going to do now? Ye got a family?"

"I have no family, señor. I do not know."

Lone Watie watched the decision forming in Josey's eyes. He had sided the outlaw in gunfights, fled beside him ahead of posses, slept with him on the trail. He knew Josey Wales, beneath the hardness. Now he stepped to Josey's side, laying a hand on his shoulder. "Ye cain't think of takin' thet one-armed peon along. Ye got to have gun backin', Josey, *real* gun backin'."

"I've rid through Chihuahua," Travis Cobb drawled casually. "Know that neck o' Mexico. I . . ."

"Diantre! Hell!" Miguel spat. "It is me who knows Chihuahua, you damn gringo. You know nothing. It is . . ."

"You goddamned chili bean greaser," Travis snarled,

"me and Chato has stepped in every cowshit pile in Chihuahua. We pushed cows . . ."

Chato fixed Miguel with a cold stare of pity. "I was *born* in Chihuahua, you peon idiota! Like the back of my hand—every village, hacienda—I can find Escobedo as easily as mi pene. I . . ."

"Shet up," Josey said evenly. He chewed for a moment with measured meditation. "Fust off, we cain't take too many guns away from the womenfolk. They got to be *good* guns. Lone, ye'll stay, with Miguel and Travis."

There was no protest. The men studied the ground—except Chato, hitching his gun belt and watching Josey's face expectantly.

"I'll take Chato," Josey said, and tossed a nod at Pablo, "and this here farmer. Soon's he learns he ain't a yard hound—thet won't take long—he'll do."

He whirled on Pablo. "And I ain't no damn *see-norh*. It's *Josey*, ye understand?"

"Si, Sen—Josey," Pablo said hastily, "and I will go."

Chato looked at Pablo with disgust. "No one asked you —comprendes?"

"Ye know what to do," Josey said. "Git hosses fer Chato and Pablo that'll stay with mine. Hang a .44 on Pablo; he can handle it better'n a rifle. Vamoose!"

He walked away, into the house.

It wasn't easy, finding horses capable of staying with the big roan of Josey Wales. Each man carried a stiff looped lariat into the horse corral and made his own selection. They argued, pointing out weaknesses in the other's choices, but finally settled on a Morgan-chested gray for Chato, for Pablo a mean-looking grulla.

Rolled blankets, grub, and grain for the horses went behind the saddles.

Josey came from the house, holding Jamie, his arm around Laura Lee. As she took the baby from him, he kissed her long, full on the lips, and she whispered, "Ye'll take care, Josey."

"I will," he said. He pulled Little Moonlight close, her arms tightly about his neck, and squeezed Granma as she kissed his scarred cheek.

Granma was lifted from the ground by Chato as she hugged him. "Put me down, ye crazy Mexican," she protested. Chato laughed and slapped her narrow bottom. "By God!" Granma said, but she was pleased, and tears made her eyes twinkle.

The men shook hands silently, not forgetting Pablo. Lone Watie seized Josey's hand in the iron grip of a brother.

"If'n ye're not back quick, I'm comin'."

"I'll be back," Josey said, and swung into the saddle. Atop the giant roan, he looked a deadly figure. Twin-holstered .44's, leg-tied; a Navy .36 beneath the left arm, under the fringed jacket; strapped before him on the saddle were two holstered .44 pistols, and two were tied behind him.

It was the one-man dreadnaught style of the Missouri guerrilla.

Chato and Josey were mounted, their horses sidling in the wind. Pablo turned to mount the grulla. He was awkward in the high-heeled boots and missed the stirrup. The grulla skittered, snorting. Granma and Travis moved to help.

"Leave him be!" Josey's voice was harsh. They stopped. Pablo caught the horse and studied it for a moment. He held the reins in his hand and crossed the hand to the saddle horn. Sticking his toe in the stirrup, he lifted and swung, almost tossing himself over its back. He held on, teetering, as the grulla crow-hopped, and finally settled in the saddle, sombrero askew on his head.

Josey grunted, whirled the roan cat-like on powerful

haunches, and with a rush, led them out of the yard, down into the valley.

Looking back, Josey saw them bunched beneath the cottonwoods: Laura Lee and Little Moonlight, Granma and Miguel, Travis Cobb and Lone Watie. They were his life, found after the death in Missouri.

He saw them raise their hands and wave, like semaphore, back and forth, slowly; and he lifted the gray hat to signal his goodbye as he disappeared around the protruding butte.

Behind him, Chato waved his sombrero, before he too vanished. Pablo looked back. Still they waved. Timidly he raised his sombrero, then with a wide arc swept it over his head. Pablo had never waved goodbye before.

The question never rose among them: should lives be placed forfeit for a tinhorn gambler named Ten Spot? They were, all of them, swept up in the loyalty code of Josey Wales. The Mountain Code.

The Code was as necessary to survival on the lean soil of mountains, as it had been on the rock ground of Scotland and Wales. Clannish people. Outside governments erected by people of kindlier land, of wealth, of power, made no allowance for the scrabbler.

As a man had no coin, his coin was his word. His loyalty, his bond. He was the rebel of establishment, born in this environment. To injure one to whom he was obliged was personal; more, it was blasphemy. The Code, a religion without catechism, having no chronicler of words to explain or to offer apologia.

Bone-deep feuds were the result. War to the knife. Seldom if ever over land, or money, or possessions. But injury to the Code meant—WAR!

Marrowed in the bone, singing in the blood, the Code was brought to the mountains of Virginia and Tennessee and the Ozarks of Missouri. Instantaneously it could change a shy farm boy into a vicious killer, like a sailing hawk, quartering its wings in the death dive. It was the Code of the "Boys," the Missouri guerrillas that shocked a nation.

Josey Wales was conceived of the Highland Code, born of the Tennessee mountain feud, and washed in the blood of Missouri.

It all was puzzling to those who lived within a government cut from cloth to fit their comfort. Only those forced outside the pale could understand. The Indian—Cherokee, Comanche, Apache. The Jew.

The unspoken nature of Josey Wales was the clannish code. No common interest of business, politics, land or profit bound his people to him. It was unseen and therefore stronger than any of these. Rooted in human beings' most powerful urge—preservation. The unyielding, binding thong was loyalty. The trigger was obligation.

Kelly the bartender, schooled in human nature that whiskey reveals across the bar, recognized the Code, and so died content in his sure promise to Capitan Jesus Escobedo.

They rode. Josey leading, lifting the powerful roan into a slow lope across the desert. He did not lead them southeast, toward Santo Rio, but straight south, to the Rio Grande.

Cactus and mesquite straggled through the sagebrush. Spanish daggers and spiked ocotillo lent a fierceness to the dead land. The wind strummed a monotonous low chord.

They did not pause in the quick darkness after sunset; but Josey slowed pace in the uneven light of the stars.

It was after midnight when they waded their horses, stirrup-deep, across the Rio Grande, and entered the angry wound that was Mexico.

Mexico, 1868. Bleeding. Since Montezuma, Cuauahtome
—Cortes. The wound never closed. Now contre-guerrillas,
freshly loosed by their departed French masters, roamed
the countryside. Armies of bandidos. Rurales, scalping,
looting, raping, with fantastic orgasms of torture.

It was worth a man's life, taking his eyes from the
horizon to pick a flower.

The gachupin, born in Spain, looked jealously down on
the criollo—of Spanish blood, but born in Mexico. These
were the hacendados, the hidalgos, who plotted against
each other, against the peon, and held their baronages
with cunning claws of tribute and death.

The criollo looked down on the mestizo, of mixed
Spanish and Indian blood, but hired him to herd his cattle.
At the bottom, the Indian peon, who hoed the corn.

Now. Por Dios! An Indian peon in the chair of El
Presidente! The inscrutable Zapotec, Benito Juarez. Suspi-
cion spread like a haunting shadow over Mexico. The
Church bureaucracy deepened the shadow.

Juarez meant to confiscate the millions of Church-
owned acres and give them to the peon. Juarez was a
pagan. Bishops bribed generals to issue pronunciamentos
against Juarez.

The hacendados bought scalps, as did the state governors, from Rurales, from bandidos. Any scalps. So long as
the scalp was not their own. Death quieted unrest. People
do not think of land when there is terror.

Comanches hit in whirlwind seasonal raids. There was
the stealthy, never-ending horror of the Apache. Mexico
was bleeding.

They pulled their saddles in a narrow arroyo. Hidden
from eyes of the prairie, they rubbed the tired horses and
grained them. Pablo clumsily, pulling the saddle, caring for
the grulla. He was not helped.

They stretched, rolled in blankets on the ground, horses'

reins tied around their wrists. They did not eat. A war party—revenge, rescue, guerrilla-fashion.

It was cold in the first hint of dawn. Josey toed Pablo from his blanket. Chato was already saddling. Now Chato took the lead, turning southeast in a half loop, looking to cut a trail four days old, a trail of fifty horses. They ate jerked beef and cold biscuits as they rode.

Cortes described Mexico to the King of Spain by wadding a sheet of paper and tossing it before him. It was a good description. Jagged. Rocks rose bare-boned. Deep canyons cut suddenly across the prairie floor. Angular buttes. Jumbled boulders, bigger than houses, perched on the inclines of arroyos.

The morning passed, raising heat waves from the rocks, and baking the constant wind to an oven breath. They did not stop at noon.

Sometimes Chato was forced to leave their southeasterly course, searching for ways into and out of canyons and around insurmountable walls of bare butte.

It was late afternoon when they pulled up on the rim of canyon cleaving the prairie three hundred feet deep. Chato pointed to the narrow floor far below them.

"A trail, Josey," he said, "leading south."

Josey hooked a leg around his saddle horn and cut a tobacco plug. He chewed slowly, scanning the prairie. There was nothing. No sound in the late afternoon. Even the wind had diminished to a thin, whistling persistence. He spat over the canyon rim.

"Let's git down and see."

They turned south, a mile—two—and found a slope in the canyon wall. It was hot in the breathless canyon, working the horses slowly down the slope. They rested in the shadows on the floor.

Chato was first down, walking back, then forward on the trail.

"It is here, Josey," he said, "the tracks. Forty, maybe fifty horses, all shod. They are three—could be five days old. See the dung; it crumbles."

Josey did not dismount, but scanned the rim above them.

"Reckin it's Escobedo," he said quietly, "and gone south."

Chato was kneeling, studying the tracks. Now he came back and there was none of the reckless humor in his face. He looked soberly at Josey. "There are other tracks, following Escobedo. Maybe a day ahead of us."

"What kind be they?" Josey asked.

"They are not horse tracks. They are moccasin. Many of them," Chato said, "the track of the Apache."

5

It was an old trail. Narrow and worn deep in the red rocks of the floor. Centuries of Indians had passed over it, a main artery leading south.

The guerrilla instinct of Josey Wales spaced their riding. He led, Chato fifty yards behind, Pablo in the rear. One does not bunch his riders in tight places.

He watched the rim high above them. The light died. Without reflected light from the prairie, the canyon was black, and Josey whistled Chato and Pablo closer. Alertness now depended upon ear. Separating the hollow echoes of the horses' hoofs, consigning that sound to routine, pushed back in the mind—leaving silence for the nerves to ponder.

It was the water sound that brought Josey to a halt. A light gurgle somewhere in the rocks. They found it in a slit arroyo breaking the canyon wall, a stream no bigger than a man's finger dribbling from the rocks. Pablo learned: horses come first.

Filling their hats, they watered the horses, unsaddled and rubbed them with blankets. While the horses ate grain from the nose bags, Josey carefully lifted their feet, feeling for pebbles that could lame.

Only then did the men eat, sparsely on salt bacon, jerked beef; and slept as before, with reins wrist-tied.

The canyon floor lifted as they rode in pre-dawn light. By the time sun tinged red on the rock faces, they were out on a treeless plateau. The tracks of the Rurales were closely bunched, meandering through chaparral and mesquite; beside them, the relentless moccasin prints.

Despite rising heat, they slow-loped across the plateau. Sweat ringed the saddle blankets and made rivulets in the dust on the horses' legs.

Once they stopped, at noontime, to blow their mounts.

"We are doubling their pace," Chato said, pointing to the tracks. "See, their horse tracks are flat, not heel-dug. They are walking. The Apache . . . ," he pointed to a moccasin print, "they are still running—the toe is dug heavy in the ground. They can outlast a horse—diablos on a trail."

With slow calculation, Josey looked at the trail. "Wonder why them Apache are hot-trailing Escobedo?"

Chato shrugged. "Quien sabe? Who knows? They love to kill."

It was midafternoon when the trail dipped over the plateau, leading into a shallow valley. A river coursed, twisting in the valley depth, and beside it, a town.

It was not a simple Indian village, but had a cathedral

spire, and was laid out plaza-style, ringed with adobes. The Apache tracks turned away from the trail.

They dismounted, squatting on the slope as they studied the town. Josey pointed. "The corral, back of that there building, is holding fifteen, maybe twenty hosses and mules. Escobedo ain't there, fer I see no more hosses about."

"The town is Saucillo," Chato said. "I have been there many times. The building is policia. There would be ten, maybe fifteen Rurales stationed there."

Josey straightened. "We'll ring the town, till we come behind a livery barn. The hosses need some cooling, rubbing down, watering and graining. We'll stay with the hosses till we put bottom back in 'em. Then we'll see what we can find out as to do with Mr. Escobedo."

They walked the horses, sloping to the town; and Pablo had just listened again to the guerrilla, who always seeks the edge: hosses first.

The wide aisle of the livery barn was cool and dim, refreshing to man and beast. The old wrangler was profuse with gracias and polite bows, accepting the gold double-eagle from Josey. He set the stable boys to work on the horses, and then nervously joined them.

Such horses! The roan, magnifico! No such horses could be owned, except by patróns, or politicos—or bandidos. These hombres were neither politicos nor patróns.

One, dressed fancily in black with the ivory-handled pistola, waited on haunches at the street door, smoking a cigarillo. He watched the street and the wrangler with cat eyes of suspicion.

At the other door, the one-armed Indian, dark— perhaps a Zapotec, or a Yaqui, the vicious kind—followed him with an even stare that showed nothing.

And the Anglo with the sombrero of the Rebel gringos and cruel scarred face, he paced the aisle, pistolas grandes swinging on his legs, and hovered over the horses, instruct-

FORREST CARTER

ing the boys to wet blankets and rub the legs, the chests, the backs of the horses. Such care and preparacion!

The wrangler was filling grain sacks, feeling the gold coin in his pocket, when the realization suddenly struck his dull mind. He crossed himself. Then the greed began to nip.

Josey did not see him motion the ragged stable boy to his side and whisper; nor the boy slip out through the window.

And so they waited, ticking away minutes that were precious, letting the horses cool and rest. Finally they led the horses out onto the cobblestones of the plaza, walking three abreast.

The afternoon was late, bringing out señoritas who promenaded around the plaza under watchful eyes of duenas, gossiping on benches.

Through the plaza, walking, the horses' shoes ringing hollow on the stones, they turned down a street of shops and cantinas. The cantinas were coming to life in the soft dusk of evening.

They were not looking for them, and so missed the posters nailed at the corners of the plaza: the scar-face of Josey Wales. $7500 REWARD. DEAD. Nor had they any way of knowing that Captain Jesus Escobedo had left behind ten of his Santo Rio Rurales, taking the ten regulars of Saucillo with him.

They sought information on Escobedo; and the liquid, haunting guitar notes, floating through batwing doors, made them loop-tie their horses and stroll into the Cantina de Musica with scarcely a look behind them.

A single window faced the street and gave small light to the low-ceilinged room. A door to the side was curtained with stringed beads. Another door stood open at the back, where a mule was visible, cropping bunch grass. Flies buzzing over a dozen pulque-yeasted tables, the guitar notes, were the only sounds.

[46]

The cantinero behind the bar slop-sandaled forward to confront them. His face was fat, sullen, and he wiped the bar in the universal salute of bartenders.

He did not look up. "Tequila, mi amigo!" Chato shouted good-humoredly, and slapped the bar, flipping his sombrero back to hang by the thong about his neck.

Three bottles and glasses were set before them. The cantinero did not raise his eyes, and the outlaw senses of Josey Wales raised small hairs on his own neck. He looked keenly at the fat face as he spun a double-eagle on the bar.

"Escobedo?" he asked softly. The cantinero looked blankly at him and made no effort to answer.

Chato took a long swallow from the bottle. "Capitan de Rurales, Escobedo—sabes?"

"No . . . sé de Escobedo." The cantinero was placing silver change on the bar and did not look at Chato. The guitar notes died.

A woman came from behind the beaded curtain and laid a guitar on the bar next to Chato. She was full-blown. Breasts brown and ripe, hanging heavily. Crow-black hair brushed below the bare shoulders, and pock scars on her face gave a suggestive sensuality.

She knew her mark, and sided Chato without hesitation. Josey was pouring tequila into a glass. She slid a hand under Chato's shirt and rubbed his back.

"Tequila?" Chato asked politely, and shoved the bottle toward her.

"Si, caballero, si!" She seized the bottle by the neck, turned it up, then wiped her lips, wet, full, on Chato's cheek.

The slitted skirt revealed a strong thigh and olive hips. Chato slipped a hand under the slit and rubbed experimentally. Firm and muscled. She giggled. He turned to Josey with studied thoughtfulness. "You comprendes, Josey? The Rurales would have been here. They would have told her where they were going. Perhaps if I questioned her, alone, for a moment, I could discover . . ."

Josey downed the drink and sucked his teeth at the fiery liquid. "Yeah," he drawled, "I'm shore ye could. But don't take yer spurs off—ain't got the time."

Pablo blushed darkly and stared at the tequila he had poured into his glass.

Chato pulled again at the bottle and looked philosophical. "It is difficult to reason," he said. "I have been following the cows so long—always you follow them; and the lean-rumped cows are the culls—no bueno. The heavy-rumped cows are the unos buenos—perhaps that has made me what I have become, with confirmacion, a rump man."

"Yeah," Josey said drily, watching the cantinero move away to the end of the bar. "I kinder noticed that—ye and Travis—ye smell a little cowy too. I'll jest keep this here tequila. Git on with yer questioning."

Pablo downed the drink, like Josey, in one gulp. He wheezed, spat, coughed and bent double. Josey beat him on the back.

"Come, querida." Chato flung an arm about the neck of the woman and staggered only slightly as they passed through the beads.

Pablo was gasping. He leaned an unsteady elbow on the bar and tears ran down his face. "I—I am sorry, Josey," he said, and Josey watched the slight jerk of the cantinero's head at the name.

"That's all right, son," he drawled. "Drinking's the last thing ye got to learn." He didn't show the alarm racing through his mind. The bartender knew—knew the name, Josey Wales!

A steady squeak of bed springs came through the curtain beads, then short woman-cries.

"By God," Josey said, "I'm glad Granma ain't here."

"Me too," Pablo muttered. Pablo meant it.

They came without warning. Four through the front door, three in the back. Heavy pistols hanging on their hips. Some of them had not yet peddled the scalps. Hair hung from belts and vests. Rurales.

"Git away from me," Josey whispered venomously at Pablo. "Take a bottle. Git to a table at the side." Pablo grabbed a bottle and slipped quickly from their path.

They lined the bar on each side of Josey. The cantinero, without speaking, placed bottles before them. A stench filled the room, acrid in Josey's nostrils: dried blood, stinking bodies, horse sweat.

Easily, almost lazily, he took a bottle in one hand, a glass in the other, and casually moved from the bar, sauntering toward the shadowed center of the room.

The Rurales drank with gusto, smacking lips, watching Josey with canny eyes of triumph, wiping drooping mustaches and beards with the backs of their hands.

They did not notice being placed in the light of the two doors, the scar-face bandido in the center shadows; a very slight edge, but nevertheless an edge, for the professional pistolero.

The squeaking bed springs stopped. Pablo sat down at his table.

They turned, all as one, facing Josey. Smiling. Cunning smiles of double meaning, always reducing victims to quivering cowards. The leader, standing in their center, doffed his sombrero in mock politeness and held it before him. His smile grew broader, white teeth overbiting his lower lip. "Señor! We welcome you to our country. We . . ."

Josey Wales returned the smiles—it was meant to be a smile. They could not see his eyes, shadowed beneath the wide-brimmed hat; but the smile trenched the scar, deep and livid, giving a lynx effect of evil cruelty. The Rurales stiffened at the sight of such a man.

Josey spread his arms wide, holding the bottle and the glass. "See-norhs . . ." His voice carried the unmistakable whine of the frightened victim; the Rurales relaxed. "I ain't looking fer trouble. I was . . ."

The bottle and glass fell from his hands. Long before they touched the floor, a big Colt appeared magically. Josey Wales was fanning.

He shot the leader through the sombrero, dead center, the heavy .44 slug knocking him backward into the bar. The deep-throated pistol was fired staccato, so rapidly, it was solid sound. The face of a Rurale smashed, fountaining blood. Another twisted, head down in crazy floppings.

Josey dodged to his left, kicked against the 'dobe wall, like a ballet dancer, back toward the center of the room, fire belching from the barrel of a second Colt in his left hand as he moved.

One Rurale cleared leather, and flipped forward as he cleared, jolted by a low hit.

From behind the beaded curtain, another revolver opened up, rapid-fire. The room shook with the thunder. Smoke fogged the air. Pablo had jerked the pistol from his holster and was firing.

His first shot killed the unsuspecting mule behind the rear door, knocking it kicking in the sand. His second shattered bottles behind the bar. Getting the range, his third knocked the leg from under a Rurale.

Through it all, a wild scream rose, carrying upward, almost beyond the range of human voice, and fell, broken cries of inhuman exultation. The rebel yell of Josey Wales.

Two Rurales broke for the rear door. One made it, fleeing the sound and the blood-crazed killer. The second fell, his back blown out between the shoulders.

It was over in thirty seconds. Chato stood, naked from the waist down, outside the beaded curtain, pistol in hand.

Blood ran unnoticed from his side. Pablo, dangling the big pistol in his hand, looked dumbly at the carnage of bodies.

Josey Wales was over the bar, cat-quick, and yanked the cantinero to his feet. He shoved the barrel of a Colt into the fat throat. "Escobedo!" he snarled, and cocked the hammer.

The heavy face broke in sobs, "Por Dios! Por favor! He rides to Escalon! Escalon! Escalon!"

"He is speaking truthful." Chato spoke quietly, cold sober. "The woman, she say the same thing."

Josey crashed the pistol barrel across the head of the cantinero. He fell limp in the blood of his skull.

Josey inspected Chato's wound. " 'Tain't much," was his curt remark. He cut a tobacco plug. "Reckin we'd better be gittin' along." Chato hurriedly pulled on his pants and boots.

Josey was tilting bodies of Rurales with his toe. "Pablo," he called, "go through their pockets. Put everything on the bar."

Pablo holstered the pistol and bent, a little reluctantly, to the job. There were six of them, sprawled bloodied and smashed by the ponderous slugs of the .44's.

"This one," Pablo indicated a Rurale lying spread-eagle on his back, "is alive."

Josey walked to him and looked down. The Rurale was conscious. He had been hit in the stomach. The stench of torn intestines mingled with the sweetish odor of blood.

"Was ye at Santo Rio?" Josey asked quietly.

The Rurale grinned faintly. "SI!" he said boastfully, surprisingly strong. The grin twisted meanly. He reached a hand into the pocket of his leather jacket and drew forth a sparkling object. It dangled from his hand, swinging.

"Si . . . puta!" and he laughed, coughing. It was an earring, Rose's. The left-hand Colt slid easily upward in

Josey's grip, cocked as it cleared leather. He shot the
Rurale between the eyes and watched him string-jerk with
the sudden shock. He spat tobacco juice into the blank
face.

Pablo had cleaned their pockets. A small mound of gold
and silver coins lay on the bar.

"Halve it," Josey said, "you and Chato."

"But . . ." Pablo protested.

"It's gun law, son; onliest kind we can live by," Josey
said evenly, "and ye done right well, son."

The vaquero and the peon halved the coins. Josey
selected a double-eagle from the pile and flipped it to the
naked woman, standing at the beaded curtain. Her face
was impassive, stoic.

"That's fer the—question," he said, "and ye tell 'em
Josey Wales and his friends done this—fer Santo Rio—
understand?"

"Si, gracias," she answered, not smiling. She caught the
coin and crossed herself quickly for the bandido who had
no soul.

They rode, galloping through the cobblestoned plaza of
Saucillo. Every door closed, windows shuttered.

To the south, they turned the horses, galloping, deliberately pacing.

Somewhere ahead of them, frightened horsemen were
running their horses to death. Josey Wales! The blood-
crazed bandido was riding wild in Mexico!

6

In the twilight, deepening toward night, they galloped out of the river valley and up onto the vast Chihuahua plain. The southward trail toward Escalon drifted through cactus and mesquite.

Here, gamma grass grew in bunches so sparse it required forty acres to feed a cow, and many rancheros numbered their cattle in the tens of thousands; here, a Don measured his land not by acres, but how many days were required to cross it.

A neighbor's hacienda could be a hundred miles or more, and the cattle ran wild as the pumas, only occasionally rounded up by the vaqueros, who were wilder than the cattle.

It was the land of Chato Olivares, unbridled and reckless, soaking its aimless existence into the soul of a man like an incense, until it owned him, and made him, and presented him to the towns as its spirit—the vaquero.

There was no moon. The night dropped its blanket and the wind turned cold. Chato led, slackening the pace, and it was he who whistled softly as he brought his horse to a halt. "There are not as many tracks, Josey," he said as Pablo and Josey reined in beside him. "It is dark, but somewhere, they have turned aside. They are not on the trail to Escalon."

Josey's saddle creaked as he shifted weight. "Where? Where'd he be a-goin'?"

Chato shrugged in the darkness. "Maybe west to Coyamo, maybe northwest to Casa Grande. He is making a swing perhaps of his territory; but he is not going on the trail to Escalon. Quien sabe? It is too dark to tell."

Pablo's voice shook slightly. "But the riders, the Rurales who escaped, they will know. They are riding ahead. Capitan Escobedo will discover that we follow."

"Yeah, I know," Josey said; a faint touch of bitterness was in the words. He knew. Like it had been in Missouri and Kansas; always, the countryside up in arms. Where a man rode with his nerves tingling on his fingertips. Where he shot at the bush that did not wave as it should in the wind.

Now they would know. His stomach hardened, holding down the sickness of Missouri, tightening the nerves for the madness of the death game to come.

They sat their horses, stomping impatiently in the wind. Chato felt helpless, that somehow he had failed; but no one could fight the darkness.

It was Josey who broke the silence. "I figger," he said, "them yellers thet broke and run will tell tall tales to Escobedo. Might be it'll keep Escobedo running, and, if it's like ye say, Chato, Escobedo wants to put on a big show; maybe it'll buy some time fer Ten Spot . . ." His voice trailed away and he squinted his eyes at a star breaking the cloud cover. "We'll backtrack a mile er two; pull off the trail. Wait fer light."

Breathing hope into their hopelessness, he led them back up the trail and off it, into the brush. He unsaddled the roan, away from Chato and Pablo, haltering him to munch the gamma grass and tying the end of the tether to his saddle horn.

Pulling a Colt, he held it across his stomach as he stretched on the ground, head on saddle and hat tilted over his eyes. The eyes did not count now, only the ears and the ground-feel. The roan would snort at an undue presence. The sudden jerk of his head would pull the saddle.

Josey had not mentioned that Escobedo would now set up the ambuscades. Chato knew already; and Pablo—there was no need for his knowing.

He saw the wounded Rurale waving the earring of Rose tauntingly before him, and briefly, the picture flitted back to Missouri, of long ago—his smoldering cabin, the charred skeleton of his wife and his boy—this he had seen when he shot the Rurale between the eyes.

He swallowed the bitterness in his throat and drifted lightly into the restless sleep of the outlaw.

Chato and Pablo tethered their horses in the same manner, as Josey had told them, separate and apart. The night wind rose, and the cactus spines delicately played a light shrieking on the wind, as of spirits far away, agonizing in an ethereal chorus.

Pablo crawled close to Chato. "Chato," he said.

The vaquero did not lift the sombrero from his face, but he whispered, "If you would talk, niño, whisper, like the wind. Sound carries far on the plains of night."

Pablo crawled closer to where Chato lay. In the distance, a wolf mourned, long and quavering. "The wolf?" Pablo whispered.

"Si," Chato answered, "but it is also the cry used by the Apache; and the Apache crosses the plains only by night."

A coyote yipped a taunting reply.

"Chato?"

"Si?"

"Was it a necesidad—I mean, Señor Josey shooting the wounded Rurale, the taking from their pockets?" Pablo asked.

Chato laughed softly. "You will never comprendes, niño. The Rurale was a torturer. He loved to see the pain in others. Josey gave him the quick death. Their pockets? They are looters of the helpless. Justice is that one shall receive what one deserves, it is the only justice—good, or bad. It is the code of the bandido, Josey Wales. Would you leave the fillings of their pockets for the puta and the cantinero?"

"No," Pablo whispered hesitantly.

"Rest easy in your mind, Pablo," Chato whispered. "The coins that jingle your pockets are justice, and the prize of war. If Josey Wales could have hauled the Rurales before a judge, the judge would take the loot, and he would divide with his politicos, and they would buy new carriages with fringes on top, and their putas would wear new rings. And Josey Wales and Pablo and Chato Olivares would be swinging from the gallows. That is their justice. Josey Wales? He has only the gun."

The silence was long and Pablo pondered the words. He began to crawl back to his saddle, for Chato was obviously asleep.

"Pablo?" the vaquero whispered.

Pablo stopped in his crawling. "Si?"

"Since you were a niño, you planted the maize, the corn, each spring in the ground. Verdad?"

"True," Pablo whispered.

"And you watched it grow, birthing with the rain from the womb of Mother Earth—and you helped, you hoed, you gathered, you savored the fruits of the kernel. Year following year. Verdad?"

"True," Pablo whispered.

"You effect the growing of the corn, but everything you effect, everything you do, has its effect upon you. The growing of the corn, and Mother Earth, have more effect on you, so that you are Pablo—a part of Her birthing and Her growing and Her fruiting, Her gentleness, Her everlasting life and living. You will live forever, Pablo. Be glad you no comprendes the storms that move across the currents above Mother Earth; for the storms come con fiero, with ferocity grande, but die quickly. They too are a necesidad, but they do not live long. So it is with Josey Wales."

"And you?" Pablo whispered after a long time. "What are you, Chato?"

The vaquero laughed softly. "Me? I am the tumbleweed that rolls with the wind. And, niño?"

"Yes?"

"If you do not sleep, and fall asleep tomorrow in the saddle when you are needed, Josey will shoot you. When I can see and count the spines on yonder cactus, we will ride."

Pablo crawled back to his saddle. He lay for a long time watching stars that winked between the scudding clouds. For the first time in his life, he was glad he was Pablo. The words of the vaquero stirred something backward through time, before his people had been yoked by the Spanish. He felt Indian.

Against his back Mother Earth felt alive. Her rains were holier than the water flicked upon him from the pot of the Spanish priest. Vaguely, drifting into sleep, he wondered if the vaquero was a pagan priest from long ago. He slept deep, and was not troubled.

Chato had been partly right in his guess of Escobedo's destination. Coyamo, to the west.

After leaving Saucillo with fifty riders at his back, Escobedo had shrugged off the peculiar haunting coldness left by the words of Kelly. Josey Wales—wild words and images spouted by a tequila-soaked cantinero. Superstition fit for a peon perhaps, but not for Capitan Jesus Escobedo.

He had not chosen Coyamo as his destination aimlessly. There was system, efficiency and ambition in the plans of Escobedo.

The rich silver mines dotted the land of this area, deep with their treasures; but the peons fled in the night; the better families would not settle the towns. Neither priest, nor prayer, nor sword could enlarge the sparse population. All for one reason. The Apache. The creeping death that raided, murdered, and used the wiles of El Diablo in their endless terror.

The Apache, like smoke in the hand; they would not stand and fight but ran for the Sierra Madre, but always, always, came back to strike again.

It was a source of great pain and embarrassment to the Governor of Chihuahua, as in all states of the north. It was of great issue in Ciudad de Mexico itself. Civilization had not only been halted by a handful of murderous animals; it was withering away.

The man of genius and planning, of action and foresight, had a future, becoming a colonel perhaps, even a general. With such power, he could share in the silver of the mines, play the game of land reform in Ciudad de Mexico with Benito Juarez, and with the other hand return the land to the Dons, and share also with them. From general to Don was not an impossible step. Don

General Jesus Escobedo! A rightful return of his name to the aristocracy to which it belonged.

There had been only two Apache bucks at the camp he and his Rurales had surprised. One had escaped. He had the other as a prisoner. Thirty-five bitches and bastardos put to the sword! He had one more Apache captive, a bitch, thirteen, maybe fourteen years of age. He had the gringo criminal.

His plan had the genius of simplicity. First, to hang the Apache buck in the town of Coyamo, to put spine in the Alcalde, the Mayor, and win praises from the mouth of the Alcalde and the Priest for his successful raid, praises that would reach the Governor and the bishops. It would demonstrate to the peons the power of his Rurales over the Apache.

From Coyamo he would travel further west to Alda-mano and there, after his own private "questioning" of the Apache bitch, she would be hanged outside the town for all to see. The praises would come from Aldamano.

Then, leaving part of his force at Coyamo, part at Aldamano, he would travel with only ten Rurales to Escalon. There, before the military, closer to Ciudad de Mexico and the people of influence, he would recount his chase of the gringo who had killed a Mexican officer of the law. How he had pursued him to the haven of criminals, Santo Rio, fought a pitched battle with the bandidos there, and returned with the criminal.

Mexico! Demonstrating to the hated gringos of the north that the long arm of Mexican justice reached even to the Rio Grande, through, of course, the dedication of Capitan Escobedo. He would tell of the slain thirty-five Apache. The newspapers in the capital would acclaim his efforts. The bishops, who even now fretted at the dwindling trib-ute income from the peons, would bring pressure to give him more authority; and the mine owners, the Dons.

Perhaps from capitan to general—it had been done before. And with the power after that—why not?—El Presidente!

Wild dreams? Not in turbulent Mexico. Even more fantastic dreams had come true. The goal of Escobedo was possible, even probable, for he was not a dreamer alone. He was a man with the attributes necessary to carry out the dreams; no moral conscience blocked his actions. The plan would succeed.

Coyamo had been rebuilt by the Spanish from an old enjido, a communal Indian village. 'Dobe hovels crowded close behind the one main street of stores and cantinas. A church had been built to christianize the Indian; and a low 'dobe wall circled the town, one of the futile gestures against the Apache.

Escobedo brought his Rurales in at sundown, columns of twos, military-fashion. They were soldados now, and under pain of death to act otherwise.

Two paces behind, and at his side, rode Lieutenant Valdez; Escobedo had only slightly concealed his contempt for Valdez' mestizo blood.

Charging Valdez to quarter the Rurales near the stables and corrals, place guardias about the town, and throw the gringo and Apache buck in jail, he retired to the private quarters reserved for the Capitan of Policia. He had the Apache girl bound by her feet and hands and left in his quarters while he paid his respects to the Alcalde and the Priest.

The Alcalde's hacienda was set back, respectably, from the street, and pleasantly patioed, with an iron grill gate. It was in the patio they ate their meal; the Alcalde, his plump wife, and the Priest in attendance to the Capitan. Indian women served the courses, shuffling back and forth to the kitchen at sharp commands of the matrona.

For a mestizo, Escobedo thought, the Alcalde showed

some knowledge of manners. True, he was hasty in his eating, hurrying to get past the pleasantries.

How had been the Capitan's patrol? The health of his family? If he needed for his troops, only ask. The fat jowls of the Alcalde trembled in the candlelight. He waited impatiently for the cigars and wine, for the retirement of his wife, before presenting his case—the excuses for his lack of progress, which threatened to break his political career and send him back to the work of a menial bootlicker.

His voice rose in a whine: The peons brought in to work would not stay. They had even tried corralling them, like horses in a stockade, but they escaped and ran in the night. They were not rebellious. They were afraid. The Apache.

Some of the mines were only partially worked. Some had closed down. If the Capitan could relay his message to the south; could station more men . . . if . . . if . . .

Escobedo had heard it all before. When was it? In 1760, the Governor of Chihuahua, answering the King of Spain's demand as to why he was not settling and progressing with his territory, offered the same excuse, as did the governors of Sonora and other states to the north. The Apache. In 1680, the same answer. The Apache.

How far back had it begun? How many political careers ruined? How many generals court-martialed? How many families of aristocracy disgraced and exiled to oblivion? The Apache.

Escobedo nodded his head in sympathy through the cigar smoke. He murmured his agreement with the waving hands of the Alcalde. He waited for the Priest to speak.

The Priest was a thin man, and wore his black robes with dignity. His face was white, esthetic, obviously not far removed from the Court of Spain. He was of a family that might have chosen to remain in the high circles of diplomacy or perhaps the military, but he had chosen the priesthood. Without question, he was a man close to God.

Though he had drunk as much wine as Escobedo and the Alcalde, his tongue was not thick, and his words were patient with forbearance. He spoke softly and with a saintly grace. "The Indian peon is good. The Church has made great progress in his Christianization. He is aware of his burden of sin and of his only deliverance. He attends the masses and rituals. He is simple; but he has a soul." The Priest paused and looked heavenward for his thoughts.

"May I be forgiven, por Dios, if I am wrong." He crossed himself with slow majesty. "But I have come to believe in my heart the Apache is an animal. He has no soul. Either this, or he represents El Diablo upon this earth. He raids even the churches of God, desecrates the sacred images and blasphemes the altars." He spoke more softly. "On two occasions, I have sought to talk with Apache captives, to tell them of love, of the word of God, to reach their souls. In their eyes I find only hate burning at my soul." The priest shuddered at the picture. "Such hate!" His voice trembled. "They have spat in my face and defamed the robe and the Cross with their spittle." He bowed his head at the hopelessness. The indignity.

The Priest, of course, made no review of history in his talk. The history of the bishops, seeing the politicos and the Dons raping the wealth of Mexico and using the slavery of the Indian, while the Church was left standing to take only the tithes of these wealthy. The bishops used their influence with the King to "end the slavery of the Indian."

The King had responded. His proclamation read that all Indians must be paid a "living wage," and he left it up to the Church and the politicos to decide what that living wage should be. The politicos controlled the price of maize and beans, and so the "living wage" fluctuated accordingly.

The Priest did not mention the peon who worked in the mines, carrying three and four hundred pounds of ore on his back up the ladders, hundreds of feet to the surface, fourteen, sixteen hours a day for the "living wage" of a daily peso.

Nor did he mention the Church required three hundred pesos to marry the peon in ceremony, a hundred pesos to christen his newborn, pesos for holy days and confessions, so that the Indian peon worked continually in debt to the Church—and to the seller of the corn, becoming not a slave of one master, but of two, enriching the Dons with the wealth of kings. And the Church now owned millions of acres of land, upon which the peon must work "free" to pay tribute to the Church. The Church, so wealthy even the federal government in Ciudad de Mexico often borrowed from its holy coffers to meet its own haggling budget, at interest, of course.

He did not mention that the average survival time of the Indian mine worker was five years, that the Church urged him to "have children and replenish the earth." He was expected to breed at least five niños before his death.

The Indian of Mexico was dying. Dying in the slow grinding that showed no violence, and wrapped in the black robe of the Church. The steel foot of greed pressed him toward his heavenly reward.

The Priest did not speak of these things. They were material matters having nothing to do with the spiritual; and above all, the Priest concerned himself with the soul of the Indian peon.

The warmth of the wine and the Priest's words and manner made the heart of Capitan Jesus Escobedo go out to this man of God.

He, Escobedo, after all was here to bring hope, safety for the Church, progress for Mexico and civilization. His personal ambition was undoubtedly spurred by these holy and national causes. He could see the destiny, the "manifest destiny" that rested on his shoulders.

He spoke softly, not boastfully, of how he and his fifty Rurales had attacked a hundred Apache, twice their number; had slain thirty-five and put the rest to rout.

One captive he would hang on the western border of Coyamo at dawn as a warning to the Apache, to give encouragement to the Christian peon. The other captive would be hanged at Aldamano, sixty miles to the west.

He recounted how he had fought the pitched battle on the very border at the Rio Grande, and won, and brought back the gringo criminal to face justice at Escalon. If only he had the authority!

He could drive the Apache into the Sierra Madre, follow him where he had never been followed before, wipe him from the face of the earth.

He felt God would be with him, he said, as servant of the holy faith and the advance of civilization.

When Escobedo had finished, the Alcalde was on his feet. "I am in support of such hombres as you, Capitan! You are the life we must have in the north. Tonight—I shall not wait for morning—tonight I shall plead your case for authority to bring about this plan. I shall send it to the state capital—yea! to Ciudad de Mexico itself!" The Alcalde was exuberant and almost danced on the stone of the patio.

The Priest spread his hands before him and studied them. "I am not a man of violence. I have opposed it," he said, "but if the sword must be raised in the cause of the Cross, then it must be raised, as in the Crusades, Capitan! I shall send my support for you to the Bishop immediately."

Escobedo kept his dignity, though the exultation rushed through him, flooding him with excitement. He stood, offering gracias for the hospitality of the Alcalde's hacienda, and kneeling humbly before the Priest for a special blessing.

As he strolled down the dusty street toward his quarters, his spirits soared. He passed the jail where the prisoners were held, and surprised the guardia on duty with a hearty "Buenas noches!"

It was not yet midnight. The Apache girl awaited his pleasures in his quarters.

Somewhere he had read of the fortunes of war, how they turned. Without doubt it was true. The name of Jesus Escobedo would soon be on the lips of all Mexico!

7

In the beginning, he had not cared. Slung across the horse, head down, seeing only the ground and hearing the Rurales as they talked and cursed riding beside him, Ten Spot had not cared.

As it had been since Shenandoah. Beautiful, green, mountain-cradled Shenandoah! His parents dead, he had lived alone. A scholar with his books and with his orchard. His apple trees that burst in the spring with delicate pinkness against their white, their fragrance that sweetened the earthy leafing of the mountain oaks and the sharpness of the pine. His apple trees!

Unabashedly they displayed the fetus of life they were bringing, tiny green nubs that took shape and rounded and grew almost to bursting with the exuberance. Often he had walked his orchard, stopping to feel them, to stroke, to rub his hands against the bulging life. He could feel their pulse, hear their breathing.

And in the autumn! The autumn with its melancholy golden light in Shenandoah. How the apples reddened; first the slightest tinge of blush; then deeper and deeper came the redness, signaling to the gods their food purpose; fat and red, and at peace in their knowing they served the cause which gave them birth. He had not loved them for their profit. He had simply loved them.

The War had passed him by. He had his world, separate from the imbeciles who ran up and down the valley, chopping at each other's throats, quarreling, blaspheming the earth with their blood.

His world was apart from the insanities of men and their mean currents of politics blowing over the earth. He could, and did, live without them.

Until Sheridan! Sheridan and his savages with their torches. Like Attila, they burned Shenandoah. Everything, every field, every home, every blade of grass or leaf of tree died in the flames of Shenandoah.

First, he had tried to stop them with words, lecturing to them, as to children. Patiently he explained he was no part of the War. He was above their quarrels. He had no place in their violence.

They had laughed and ridden by him with their torches. He had walked, then run among them, first in rage as the torches licked at his home, then pleading as the flames ate at his books. He had run among the flames, stomping at them, tossing his precious volumes into the yard until he could bear the heat no longer.

He had run after them to his orchard, but the pleading in him had drained. He had watched as the orchard, the trees, the beautiful, life-giving trees, had each become a death torch. He had watched. As the ground grass lit the trees, William Beauregard Francis Willingham had died.

Like all such men proposing to set apart from the world, he entertained not the slightest thought of rebuilding. Impractical in his separate world, he was as impractical at its destruction. He had not even kicked at the ashes, but turned away and stumbled west across the miserable Southland.

No description could fathom his bitterness. He wished for death, but could not bring himself to the technicalities by which he might bring it about.

He became a swamper in saloons, sweeping floors, emptying spittoons to pay for the whiskey. He discovered his deftness with cards, and from New Orleans, he drifted west.

He had begun to feel balm for the bitterness. Deliberately he lived with the scum of the frontier. When men sneeringly referred to him as "tinhorn," he secretly rejoiced in their contempt, as when they called him "pimp," or he woke in the morning beside the body of the coarsest whore. He was these things—all these things—and many more. This is actually what he had been all the time!

Golden Shenandoah had been a shining coin he found in the street, then lost again. It had not really been his from the beginning—he had not deserved Shenandoah! He felt the bitterness leave him.

He proved it each day, earning the contempt of the lowest at the gambling tables. He proved it in his whore-mongering, his drunken revels. This was his world. He thought of Shenandoah no more. Yes, the bitterness was gone. Empty. Emptied of feeling, except the small corner where grew the strange comradeship with Rose—illiterate, a whore with no purpose, empty as Ten Spot.

He had not cared while his head throbbed from the

bullet crease, bumping against the horse. He had not cared until they righted him to ride astride and put the rawhide thong around his neck, tied to the saddle horn of a Rurale.

To be led by the neck like an animal! The resentment rose in Ten Spot. Beside him rode the Apache, bloodied and mangled, looking neither toward nor away from him.

Ahead, the Apache girl had ridden, looped in the same manner about the neck, with the rawhide secured to the wrist of the Capitan, who led them.

When they had camped, Ten Spot and the two Apache were forced to squat, hands tied behind their backs, and watch the Rurales eating. As each finished his meal, he would rise and come over, raking the scraps of food from his tin plate on the ground before them.

Ten Spot refused to eat. The two Apache bent forward, placing their foreheads against the ground; they ate like dogs from the scraps, while the Rurales watched and roared in laughter, pointing first to one and then the other.

"Animal! Bestia! Bruto!" they shouted. The Apache, patiently, stoically, continued their groveling at the scraps. They appeared not to hear.

Now Ten Spot lay against the wall of the Coyamo jail. He was tied, feet together, hands behind his back. It was more a dungeon than a jail.

A single barred window, high in the 'dobe wall, was at ground level on the outside, and heavy stone steps led upward to the single ponderous door through which he and the Apache warrior had been thrown by the Rurales.

They had followed them down, had the Rurales; and had kicked the Apache repeatedly, laughing, crooking their necks in grotesque clownish poses while they held imaginary hanging ropes over their heads. "Muerte, Apache, por la mañana!"

So Ten Spot knew the Apache would hang in the morning.

When they had gone, he stared across at the warrior, who looked at him with unblinking eyes.

Rats began to scurry about in the straw, squeaking, and Ten Spot watched, horror mounting, as two of the huge rodents boldly climbed the chest of the Apache, licking at the blood, and began gnawing at the naked end of a protruding broken rib.

The warrior watched impassively. Suddenly he rolled and caught them beneath him. Ten Spot heard their death-shrieking. He shuddered.

His hands were swollen and numb from the tight leather bindings; but now he worked them, twisting, turning, running a finger up his coat sleeve for the thin shiv knife of the gambler.

He felt it. Slowly, slowly, he worked it downward into the clutch of three fingers. It sliced the leather like butter. He loosed his hands and sat up, rubbing life back into them. He cut the thongs of his feet. Then he crawled to the Apache.

The warrior watched, looked at the knife and back into the eyes of Ten Spot. He expected death. His eyes showed no emotion, only the peculiar glazed glow of hate.

Ten Spot cut the leather from his wrists and from his ankles. The Apache sat up quickly, still unsure.

"Hablo español?" Ten Spot asked.

"Si," the Apache answered softly.

Ten Spot shrugged, pointed at himself. "Well, I no hablo español. Ain't that a hell of a situation!" He laughed weakly.

The Apache smiled. He understood. His front teeth had been kicked out, leaving deep rutted gaps in the gums. His lips were turned outward from puffy swelling. The broken rib stuck a ragged point through his side, and his stomach and breechclout were matted with blood.

He stumbled to his feet and made no sound as his

moccasins paced around the walls. Despite his terrible physical condition, his movements were panther-smooth and graceful in rhythmic body control.

He knelt and dug in a corner. Ten Spot followed and watched him curiously. Down he dug, a foot, perhaps eighteen inches. Stone! The floor was solid stone beneath the hard-packed earth and straw.

The warrior rose and, walking below the window, leaped and grabbed the bars. He pushed with his head; barely the head squeezed through; to get a body through the narrow opening would be an impossibility. Easily, he dropped to the floor. Despite his blood loss, the Apache's strength amazed the weakened Ten Spot. Now he knew why the Apache ate the scraps.

Ten Spot could bear the sight no longer. He pulled off to him, he pushed the splintered rib back into the flesh and his coat and ripped away his shirt. Motioning the Apache tightly wound strips around his chest.

When he had finished, the Apache looked down at the bandage, back at Ten Spot. He pointed to himself. "Na-ko-la," he said simply. And then, "Gracias."

"You're welcome," Ten Spot muttered, "but it'll do you very little good, my friend. They're hanging you in a few hours."

Na-ko-la grinned. He whirled, and his boot moccasins barely slithered on the straw as he glided to the wall beneath the high barred window.

Ten Spot believed he had lost his mind, for suddenly the Apache hit himself in the mouth, hard, viciously. He cupped his hand and blood gushed into it. When his hand was full, he leaped and flung the blood on the iron bars above him and on the 'dobe wall. He repeated the blows to the mouth; this time, when he leaped, he grabbed an iron bar with one hand, drawing himself up; he flung the blood outside the window.

"What the hell!" Ten Spot whispered incredulously.
Na-ko-la came and stood before him. He held out his
hand and pointed at the knife. Ten Spot handed it to him.

He moved to the far corner of the cell and knelt. Carefully he moved the knife into the earth, cutting squares.
Slowly, with meticulous care, he lifted out the squares,
keeping the top soil separated as he set them aside. As he
removed more soil, each time in squares, down to the
stone floor, he worked faster.

"By God," Ten Spot looked, open-mouthed, "damned
if he ain't dug himself a grave." He had, almost perfectly
proportioned for his body. He handed the knife back to
Ten Spot and smiled again.

Now, untying the breechclout, he squatted, defecating a
small pile there, moving and repeating his action close to
the head of his grave.

He lay down on the exposed stone surface, fitted himself, and sat up. Legs a-spraddle, with feet laid flat, he
carefully picked up the little squares. Laying his breechclout beside himself, he shaved off the excess bottom earth
onto the cloth and set the squares over his feet. They fit
perfectly. There was no mound or even a lump betraying
the resting place of the feet. He moved to the legs, repeating the action; then reaching to the pile of his own waste,
he threw it over the ground covering his lower body.

He worked as far as his neck and, breaking a hollow
straw, placed it in his mouth and looked at Ten Spot. Ten
Spot thumped his chest with the miracle he had seen.
"Well, I'm a sonofabitch!" he said.

Na-ko-la, motioning him to place the earth over his
arms and head, whispered, "Gracias, Sonofabitch!"

"No, I'm Ten . . . what the hell!" Ten Spot knelt and
shaved the earth into the breechclout, carefully placing
the squares.

The last square to be placed was over the face of

Na-ko-la. They looked long at each other, and Ten Spot saw not hate, but warmth in the eyes of an Apache.

He placed the square, careful to break the protruding straw even with the ground. Then he lightly rubbed his foot over the grave, pressing together the tiny cut marks, and scattered straw where it had been before.

He took the breechclout and, with infinite care, dribbled its raw earth around the walls of the cell. He dropped his pants to tie the breechclout around him. As he did, a thought occurred.

"Hell," he said to himself casually, "I been having belly cramps for three days. Bet I can drizzle shit enough on that corner to keep a rat from walking in it, much less a Rurale." And he did.

He sat down across the cell, back to the wall, and laughed softly to himself. "It'll be worth a beating—even a hanging, by God, to see the faces of those Rurales when they come."

Perhaps it came from watching the Apache, in the midst of disaster, of hopeless circumstance, of death, change that hopelessness to hope, even to chance for victory over sure death.

Yes, that was it, for in the middle of death, life was flowing back into Ten Spot. Into his brain.

Carefully he slid the shiv knife back into its secret pocket. He picked up the cut thongs of leather and began to chew their ends, disguising the smooth knife cut.

Ten Spot was thinking. Despite his precarious position, he felt better about the whole goddamn thing.

8

Three Rurales escaped out of Saucillo ahead of Josey Wales. One had run from the cantina half screaming of the disaster to the two remaining at the station of policia. The three had leaped on horses and ridden west for Coyamo.

Darkness caught them before they had gone ten miles, but they did not slacken the horses' running. Behind them, they could still hear the wild screams of the blood-crazed pistolero, Josey Wales. They fancied hoofbeats in pursuit.

Halfway to Coyamo, two of them, who had unluckily leaped upon lesser horses, found themselves afoot on the plains. One of the horses, heaving for breath, fell and broke its leg. A mile further, the other simply died beneath the rider with a bursted heart.

The two stranded men, hearing the wolf howl and then answered, again and again, from all directions, did not hesitate. They pulled the pistolas from their belts and blew out their brains.

The Apache silently moved in upon them, stripping their bodies of guns and ammunition. On the belt of one they found the scalp of an Apache child. With their knives, they hacked his body to pieces. The horse with the broken leg still lived. They gathered close.

They had been running for seven days and were now without rations. The leader knelt by the horse and seized the jugular vein, as one might squeeze a hose of water. Above his squeezing hand, he cut the vein and placed his mouth to it. He relaxed his grip only briefly, to receive his ration of blood, and motioned for the next warrior to seize the vein. Each stepped forward in his turn, taking of the life ration sparsely, leaving life for his brother warrior next in line.

They had no time to butcher the horse. They cut chunks of meat from it; and as their moccasin feet resumed the muffled, ominous running, they sucked the blood from the meat and chewed its tough rawness.

The remaining Rurale, far ahead, rode a dying horse into the street of Coyamo.

Capitan Escobedo, just returned from his supper with the Alcalde and the Priest, sat on the bunk of his private quarters. At his feet the Apache girl lay. Her eyes were closed.

He was in excellent spirits and reached down, running his hand over the flat muscled stomach of the girl, felt the velvet hardness of tiny breasts.

"Perhaps, querida," he murmured, "despite my tired soul and body, I should question you tonight? Pues y que?

What of that?" He began removing his boots and was delighted that the girl had opened her eyes and was watching. Was it fear?

The pounding came on the door—loud, rude!

"Capitan!" It was the voice of Lieutenant Valdez. "Es urgente!"

Escobedo cursed. "Un momento!" he shouted back at the door. He pulled on his boots, flung open the door, then stepped backward at the mad eyes of the Rurale held between the strong arms of Lieutenant Valdez and Sergeant Martinez.

They crowded immodestly into the room. Escobedo turned away from them. Walking to his desk, he lit two more candles.

"Bring him before the light," he said crisply. The Lieutenant and Sergeant half carried the sagging figure.

The Rurale lifted his face, and his eyes showed rolling and white. Saliva dripped from his mouth. His drooping mustache trembled violently.

"Saucillo!" the Rurale gasped weakly, ignoring the necessity of addressing El Capitan. "Saucillo! Muerte! All dead!"

Escobedo stepped forward and slapped him across the face, open-handed, back-handed, until the Rurale's head fell forward. His sombrero tumbled to the floor.

Lieutenant Valdez seized him by the hair and jerked his head up to face his Capitan. Escobedo slapped him again. Gradually the whites of the eyes rolled down. The Rurale looked at his Capitan. "Josey Wales . . ." He breathed it quietly. His voice trembled and carried a haunting awe of unbelief.

At the name, Escobedo felt a coldness run through him, the coldness he had felt when he had crossed the Rio Grande. His face whitened, and he gripped the Rurale by the throat, "Que? What about Josey Wales? Speak, hombre!"

The story came in snatches: The screams of a madman as he killed! Crazed for blood! Yes, there had been more men. Two besides Josey Wales; the Indian bandido had only one arm, the other they did not see, he had shot from ambush!

Now the Rurale was crying. Tears made ropes of water, wetting his jacket. His nose ran mucus into his mouth and he coughed. Escobedo kicked him in the groin. He vomited, heaving a stenching mess on the floor, on Escobedo's boots.

"Take this perro, this dog. Tie him up, hide him. He must not be seen in Coyamo! Comprendes?" He snapped the orders at Valdcz.

The Lieutenant straightened to attention. "Si, Capitan," he said crisply.

They pushed and dragged the Rurale to the door.

"When you have done this," Capitan Escobedo said, "return here, Lieutenant! Rapido!"

"Si, Capitan!"

At the closing of the door, Escobedo rushed to his desk. He jerked a bottle of tequila from a drawer, and his hand shook uncontrollably as he poured half a glass. He downed it in one swallow. He rummaged among the papers of the desk, laying out a map of the area. His hands still trembled. Raising the bottle again, he swallowed more of the tequila.

By the time Valdez returned, he was calmed. Spreading the map between them, he pointed his finger. "Here, to our northwest, no more than ten miles, is the guarida of Pancho Morino, the bandido. Comprende?"

"Si," Valdez answered. His face was puzzled. He had never learned to follow the thinking of his Capitan. He shrugged.

"Morino," Escobedo continued, his voice rising in fever as the plan took shape in his mind, "Marino has fifteen, twenty, bandidos. He is hungry and hunted. This," Escobedo rose from the map, pointing his finger in Valdez' stolid face, "this you must do. You must ride, instante, pronto! When you approach his guarida, fire three shots, that you come in peace. Tell Morino this: I wish to make truce with him. Truce that will profit him mucho. To prove my fidelity, I will meet him in one hour from the time you talk with him, on the road west of Coyamo. I will be alone. He may send his sentinels to prove this. Comprendes?"

"Si, Capitan, but . . ."

"VAMOS!"

Valdez rushed to the door.

"And Lieutenant, you will tell no one of your mission. Have Sergeant Martinez saddle my horse."

"Si, Capitan."

Valdez hurried to the stables and galloped out of sleeping Coyamo.

Escobedo paced the floor, back and forth, in the flickering light of the candles. The panic had left him. He was at his best in a crisis. He knew it, taking pride in his quick cunning.

He had brought fifty Rurales to Coyamo with him; ten were already stationed here. Sixty men. Josey Wales would never attack sixty men. He knew the type. They moved like the coyote. Like the Apache. Wales would strike when he found a weakness—out of the dark, when Escobedo was alone; perhaps in the back. The Capitan had his plan.

He sat on the edge of the desk, swinging his leg easily in a tight circle. He ran his finger along the thin mustache and traced his sensitive chin in thought. Drinking again from the tequila, he smiled down at the Apache girl, a benevolent, even a fatherly, smile. "Perhaps tomorrow night, querida. Business before pleasure, eh?"

Her eyes were closed. Softly he pushed her stomach with his boot, but she did not open her eyes.

He knew she was making the pretense. These Apache! Really children when one with intelligence handled them!

He walked to the stables, mounted his waiting horse, held by Sergeant Martinez. Slowly he trotted the horse out the westward gate. Escobedo would keep his word. He would ride alone. This time.

For nearly an hour, he lazily trotted his mount. Now he began to hear outriders in the brush. These bandidos! They trusted no one.

In the dim light, he could spot Pancho Morino, the silver edging the sombrero, the tint of silver on his saddle. He rode with Lieutenant Valdez, and they halted their horses a few yards from each other.

"You may return to your quarters, Lieutenant," Escobedo said casually to Valdez. The Lieutenant galloped away, glad to leave the encircling riders.

Escobedo waited until the hoofbeats had died in the distance. Then he spoke, "Señor Morino, I have kept my word. I am alone."

The impassive face of the bandido showed nothing. "Si," he said shortly, and sat his horse, waiting.

The wind was rising, and Escobedo slowly walked his horse closer. He halted a few feet from Morino as the bandido's hand fell toward his holster.

"What I have to say is for our ears alone. Comprendes?"
"Si."

Escobedo breathed deeply. How to explain to this sub-human Indian peon who had gone mad?

"A gringo pistolero who calls himself Josey Wales has become a nuisance on my trail. He kills the defenseless, but runs at sight of my troops. He has only two compadres. It would be a beneficio if he was killed . . . beneficio mucho to me."

Morino's horse stomped and skittered in the wind. He brought him under control.

"So?" he said softly.

"Tomorrow," Escobedo continued patiently, "he will ride into Coyamo, but only if I am not there. At dawn this day, I and all my sixty Rurales will leave Coyamo. We will ride sixty miles to the west, to Aldamano. You may place sentinels on the road to guarantee my trust. You are a bandido. You will know how the ambuscade can be made. This is your way."

Escobedo saw the slight lift of Pancho Morino's eyebrows.

"And my profit?" Morino asked softly.

"Your profit shall be this." Escobedo paused for the effect of profit—grande. "The town shall be yours for two days. You may collect your—tribute—in that time. I will not return until two days following a messenger from you to Aldamano that Josey Wales and his compadres are dead."

He waited. The impassive Indian bandido said nothing.

"You may place sentinels on the road at all times, of course, to insure my word," he added, urgency creeping into his voice.

"And how will I know this Joh-seh Wales?" Morino asked.

Escobedo handed a poster across to Morino. "You cannot fail to know. He wears the gray hat of a gringo Rebel. His face is heavy-scarred. One of his compadres has but one arm."

Pancho Morino folded the poster. "It is done," he said.

Escobedo extended his hand. The bandido spat on the

ground. He wheeled his horse, whistled to his outriders, and was gone.

As Morino disappeared into the blackness, Escobedo breathed hard between clenched teeth, "You will pay for that insult, peon bastardo!"

The time was now short until dawn. Back in Coyamo, he ordered Valdez to mount all troops to leave at dawn for Aldamano. Hurrying to the Alcalde's hacienda, he roused the servants to the gate. He met the Alcalde, still sleep-drugged, in the patio.

"My scouts," he announced curtly, "have sighted Apache forty miles to the west. We leave immediately to encircle and destroy them. We shall be back quickly."

The Alcalde came alive. "Bravo! At this hour! I shall commend your diligence to the Governor! Vaya con Dios!" He shouted the last, for the Capitan had bowed stiffly, taking his leave like an officer off to perform his urgent duty.

The Alcalde ran to the iron gate and shouted again to the retreating back of the gallant Capitan. "The Priest will ask a special blessing for you, Capitan, for you and your brave men!"

The Capitan raised his hand in final salute that he heard, but he did not turn.

The troops were mounted. Capitan Escobedo at their head with the Apache girl, neck thonged by his side. Then he sent for the prisoners.

Flinging open the heavy cell door, four Rurales came down the stone steps. They stopped at the sight of Ten Spot sitting against the wall. Dumbly they looked about them. "En donde Apache?" one of them asked stupidly of the others.

Ten Spot laughed and pointed to the window. "He vamoosed, you silly bastards. Through the bars!"

They ran to the window, leaped up to look out, ran around the cell. Ten Spot, already weak, fell over on the floor, laughing. He held his sides. "Vamoosed, bastardos!" He gasped for air between squeals of hysterical laughter.

One of the Rurales stepped into the piles of human waste left by Ten Spot and Na-ko-la. He sniffed, lifted his boot, "Excremento!" he shouted in disgust.

Ten Spot lost his breath. He rolled on the floor, laughing uproariously. They kicked him in the head, the stomach, the face, but could not silence him.

Dragging him up the steps, they flung him, bound, astride a horse. Still his laughter sounded, echoing insanely hollow in the eerie light of dawn.

Escobedo was furious, but his fury had to be suffered in silence. The Alcalde and the Priest would forget all about the Apache when he rode back and rescued their town from the murdering bandido Pancho Morino. Si. Morino would swing just as high on a gallows.

He raised his hand, waving forward, column of twos, west to Aldamano.

And as they rode, the whispers flew down the line of Rurales. No human could have gone through the bars. Only a servant of El Diablo! Truly! The Apache was evilly sainted by El Diablo himself!

9

In that same early dawn, the tracker eyes of Chato Olivares found the trail. They had backtracked less than a half hour when he saw the tracks. There was no doubt. "Coyamo, Josey," he said, "they've gone to Coyamo. The tracks are not old. We're getting close!"

Getting close! There in the ghost light of the desert dawn, they sat their horses. Getting close. Then what?

Josey Wales cut a tobacco plug, pushed it into his cheek and thoughtfully chewed. He spat on the flat spoon of a ground cactus and noted, with passing satisfaction, the dead-center hit.

"Well," he drawled as he spurred the big roan, "let's git at it."

They took the trail to Coyamo at a ground-covering gallop. The sun rose behind them, pinking gamma grass and sparkling the cactus spines like silver needles. They kept up the hard pushing of the horses, even as the sun rose higher and raised the heat on the desert floor.

They stopped briefly at the hacked remains of the first Rurale and his horse. The buzzards were already feeding, and boldly hopped but a few paces away, already too glutted to inspire flight.

"Apache," Chato said.

" 'Pears like them fellers want to make shore they do the job," Josey said flatly. Pablo closed his eyes.

They rode on and didn't stop at what was left of the second Rurale. But they were forced to slacken the gait of the horses. For a mile they walked them.

"Wondering," Josey said, "if them was the only two got away, er if there was another un."

"No way to tell, Josey," Chato said, "the tracks are too many."

"Why?" asked Pablo.

"Well," Josey answered drily, "sometimes it makes a difference if ye know company's coming, er if it ain't."

"We being, of course, the company," Chato explained politely to Pablo.

The sun had tipped past noon when they sighted Coyamo, shimmering, flat and white, like a mirage in the desert heat.

Josey pulled up. "Reckin that's her," he said.

"Si," Chato agreed with a fatal solemnity, "that is her."

They sat for a while, blowing the horses. Josey reached back in a saddlebag and drew out the little long-glass. He handed it to Chato.

"Tell ye what ye do, Chato," he said, "ye take this glass and circle around left of that town, up on thet knoll ye see way off yonder." He nodded his head to indicate the yonder. "From there," he continued, "ye look over everything ye can, the town. When ye pull thet little glass all way out, she'll give ye twelve, fifteen mile in this country. They cain't hide hosses. Check all around."

"Si," Chato said, and took the glass.

"And Pablo," Josey said, "ye circle right of the town. Ye ride wide, look fer hosses. If ye see more than five er six, ye wave yer hat. Otherwise, both of ye ride in from t'other side of town. We'll meet at the stables. Hosses come first."

"And what will you do, Josey?" Chato asked.

Josey Wales looked surprised. "Me? Why I'm a-going to jest keep walking this hoss right on into town. Onliest way a Missouri brush rider ever learnt to do it. Git!"

They galloped their horses, Chato and Pablo, widening in arcs around the town. As they rode, Josey Wales began to walk the big roan, easy at first, then into a soft Sunday jog, like maybe he was a-going to church or social-calling on a gal. It was the way of Josey Wales.

As he rode, he watched Pablo, riding wide, down a slight dip in the prairie and up again. On his left, he saw Chato reach the knoll and stand his horse for a long time, moving the glass, scanning.

He began to talk casually, to himself and to the horse. "We've rid with some good uns in Missouri, Red. Them two there will do." He came closer and saw Chato come off the knoll and circle still further to the west. Pablo was arcing from the right.

When Josey reached the arched entrance to the town street, he never paused, but trotted in—as any oblivious pilgrim might do, he figgered.

But Josey Wales could not be mistaken for a pilgrim, even by the village idiot. The horse was the kind a man depended on for his life, and pilgrims do not ride about the countryside wearing .44 Colts tied down on their legs, with four additional Colts holstered and showing on the saddle. Pilgrims did not display the scarred grim-looking face that belonged to Josey Wales.

As he came under the archway, a blanketed Indian, leaning against the wall, ran behind the buildings. Two sombreroed peons squatting against the side of a cantina required the slightest of looks to cause their disappearance. The steady clip-clop of the big horse was the only sound.

"Right peaceful 'pearing little village, Red," Josey continued his drawling talk to the horse, "like some of them Kansas towns we used to ride into. Howsoever, I don't see no bank about." What he was saying was what he felt. There was no one on the street. It was peaceful.

He rode past a cantina where three horses were hitch-railed, resting three-footed in the hot sun. The middle horse was a huge dappled black with silver-trimmed saddle and stirrups.

"Now that un," Josey drawled to his horse, "that un there might give ye a run, Red." The big roan pricked his ears and snorted his disgust. Three horses, no more. The town was empty. A storekeeper stood back in the shadows and watched him pass.

He saw the livery barn, wide-aisled, and took the roan in without dismounting. Chato and Pablo were there already.

"Through the glass," Chato said, "es nada, empty as far as I can see."

"Si," agreed Pablo, "nada."

There was no one in the big barn. The stalls showed one mule and a jackass, old and sleeping.

"Reckin we can grain and cool these hosses," Josey said.

They stripped the saddles. Rubbing down the horses, they gave them only a little water. Then from a grain bin they filled nose bags and put them on the horses. They filled their own grain bags, to be slung behind saddles, and had just turned from this when a man walked into the shade of the wide aisle.

Josey quickly motioned Pablo to the back door. The man wore the boots and spurs of a vaquero, but his dress was the poor sackcloth of the peon.

He stopped and politely lifted the straw sombrero, holding his arms wide to show he carried no guns. He was dark-skinned, with a prideful mustache that drooped below his jaws.

He smiled and bowed. "Buenas tardes, señores," he said softly.

"Buenas tardes," Chato answered.

"I reckin," Josey drawled, and squatted on his heels.

"Muy . . . ," the stranger began.

Josey turned to Chato. "Tell him to talk to you. Ye'll tell me, and then we'll all know what in hell he's got on his mind."

Chato spoke rapidly in Spanish. The man smiled and nodded his agreement.

Hesitantly at first, then more rapidly, he talked, continually smiling. Josey figgered he was apologizing for something. When he had finished, Chato turned to Josey. His face was a shade whiter, his lips drawn.

"He say," Chato began, "that his leader is Pancho Morino. He say Pancho Morino is a great pistolero—and he *is*, Josey, *mucho* grande. He has killed many men. He say Pancho Morino is up the street in a cantina, and has heard you are Josey Wales, a pistolero grande. He say Pancho would like the honor of meeting you in the street to contest which is more grande." Chato stared at the ground. Then: "That's all he say—except, if you win, we all ride free of his twenty bandidos; you lose, then we—Pablo and me—we die too."

"Which way is the cantina?" Josey asked.

Chato asked the question and was answered. The man

pointed back toward the east, where the three horses were hitch-railed.

Josey cut a tobacco plug and chewed meditatively. He spat, rolling a confused dung beetle in the manure of the aisle. "Tell this here feller," he said slowly, "that I have heerd of what a great pistolero he is—which I ain't—but tell him that bullshit anyhow. Tell him I know that him being a great hoss man, he understands I got to see to my hoss fust off. Tell him I'll send a messenger up the road there in a few minutes to the cantina, unarmed, to let him know as what is most convenient, all around . . . Reckin that's all."

Chato related the message in fluid Spanish, leaning heavy on the "grande" when he spoke of Pancho Morino. When he had finished, the man bowed politely, turned and walked from the stable.

"Josey," Chato said, "this Pancho Morino is very, *very* fast. He is feared over a great area. He . . ."

"Hesh up," Josey drawled, "I'm thinking." He chewed for an eternity, it seemed to Pablo. Then: "Ye know, thet's a purty hunk of hoss, that dappled black of his'n. Tell ye what—when ye go up there . . ."

"Me?" Chato asked, alarmed.

"Yeah," Josey said, "when ye go up there, tell him all that stuff 'bout me figgerin' that since we're pistoleros and sich, it'd be a sporting proposition if the one come out uppers takes the other's hoss. He's seen mine, riding by the cantina."

"Por Dios, Josey!" Chato pleaded. "Is all you thinking of *horses*?"

"Nooooo," Josey said absently, "I'm thinking something else. When ye go, tell him it'll take me 'bout a hour to git my hoss and sich in good shape." Josey squinted at the sun. "Yep," he said confidently, "hour ort to do it. And Chato, when ye go, study how he hangs his gun. Where he wears it, sich as that . . . Reckin that's all. Shuck yer gun belt and I'll hold it fer ye."

With reluctant slowness, Chato unbuckled his pistol belt. He looked longingly at it for a moment, and with the fatalistic shrug of the vaquero, he walked out of the barn toward the cantina, his jingling spurs dragging in the dust.

Josey turned to Pablo, seated at the back door of the barn.

"Pablo," he called softly.

"Si?"

"Tell ye what ye do, ye git out thet pistol and hold it in yore lap. Takes ye a shade to git it out. If ye let anybody sneak up and kill us from behint—I'll kill ye."

"Si, I will watch closely, Josey." He pulled the big pistol and laid it across his legs. Nothing moved.

The minutes dragged by; half hour. Chato reappeared, flipped his sombrero on the ground, and flopped, his back against a stall. He wiped sweat from his face. Josey squatted patiently. He handed Chato his pistol and belt.

Chato began, "First, Josey, I would never do such as that for anybody else. Remember, next time I want to borrow ahead of the wages. Second, he is the born killer. He cares nada if he dies. He has no fear. He say he has killed eighteen men he know of. He say the hour is all right." Chato paused and wiped his brow.

"Was he drinking?" Josey asked casually.

"Si," Chato answered, "from a bottle of tequila." He looked slyly at Josey. "I had two, maybe three, un poco —just little ones—to learn more, you see . . ."

"Yeah, I see," Josey drawled. "How's he hang his pistol? Sich as that?"

Chato pointed his finger at Josey. "Only once before have I see such a pistol rig—it was fast. He wears a swivel holster."

"Swivel holster? Never heerd tell of sich," Josey said.

"Some pistoleros on the border use them," Chato explained. "The pistol belt has a little knob on it, the holster swings on the knob. The pistola is never pulled from the holster. It is tied into it. The bottom of the holster is open. All he do, Josey . . . ," Chato's voice dropped in doom, "is drop his hand on the handle and thumb the hammer, up come the bottom of the holster, and BAM! She fires. He shoot from the hip, very fast . . . You see, the holster is not tied down . . ."

"Yeah," Josey interrupted, "I see." He scratched the stubble of beard on his jaw. "Is thet there holster tight agin' his hip, er hang loose, kinder?"

Chato frowned, remembering. "It is tight to his hip. It would be a necesidad, you comprendes—the leverage to push down—it could not be loose."

"Figgers," mused Josey Wales.

Chato was nervous. "How do we know when the hour has passed. We have no watch. I could not tell the time if we had one."

Josey squinted through the door at the sun. Where the shade was moving back from the corner of the barn aisle, he drew a line in the dirt with his finger. "When she gits there," he said, "reckin that'll make a good Missouri hour. Ye can wake me up then."

"*Wake you up?*" Chato nearly shouted. "You are going to *sleep?*"

"Well," he said apologetically, "if one of ye is sleepy, I'll split the watch with ye. There ain't but two doors to watch—half and half. How about it?"

"*Sleep?*" Chato exclaimed. "I could not sleep if I was dead!"

"Nor could I sleep, Josey," Pablo agreed.

Head on saddle, hat pulled over his face, Josey spraddled in the aisle of the barn. The restless sleep of the outlaw trail was different. Now he would rest between two friends.

In a moment, Chato exclaimed softly to Pablo, "Sonofa-dog! When Josey *really* sleep, he *snores!*"

And so he did.

The shade crawled quickly for Chato. He watched it, fascinated by the speed of an hour. As it touched the line in the dirt, he shook Josey.

"It is time," he said quietly. Josey stood, yawned, and stretched his body. He flexed his arms, his hands, pulled the big pistols and inspected their loads, then slid them up, down, in the holsters.

He called Pablo and Chato to his side as he stepped to the barn door. "Tell ye what ye do. Chato, ye'll walk agin' the buildings on my right side, four, five steps behind and watch the tops of the buildings, and the alleys *acrost* the street from ye. Pablo, ye'll walk same, agin' the buildings on my left. But ye watch the tops acrost the street, and the alleys. Ye see something looks like it ain't made in Granma's kitchen, ye shoot at it."

"This man," Chato said firmly, "wants a pistol duel. He is not thinking of such."

"Yeah, I know," Josey drawled. "Rec'lect several fellers died of back trouble, thinking the same thing. Ye all watch them buildings. I'll do the acquainting with Mr. Pancho."

They stepped into the street. Josey walked to the middle of the dusty street, before he turned to face east. A three o'clock sun was at his back, broiling hot.

With a pace of excruciating slowness, he strolled toward the cantina. He had measured ten steps when Pancho Morino stepped through the batwing doors, walking to the center of the street.

Turning, he brought his sombrero down to better shade his eyes. Behind him, his two men walked.

All in black he was dressed. Silver trimmed the sombrero, made shining flowers on the tight vest, ran in curling bright loops down the tight britches that flared, vaquero-style, at the boots. The single pistola, he wore high. It was ivory-handled.

Josey calculated the distance as they walked toward one another. He stopped with twenty paces between them. Morino seemed disappointed. He took another step, but Josey would not move. Morino stopped.

His face was thin, angular, dark, with a slim mustache neatly trimmed. The eyes were reckless eyes, black and flippant with their taunting look at death. He was smoking a cigar.

For a full thirty seconds, they stood. Pancho Morino broke the silence. He smiled, good-humoredly, white teeth showing in the sun. "Buenas tardes, Señor Josey Wales." Though polite, his tone was faintly mocking.

"Same to ye, Mr. Pancho Morino," Josey said lazily.

Morino was puzzled by this man. True, he appeared to be an hombre malo, scar-faced, two tied-down pistolas. For a pistola grande, however, he did not stand as all others had stood who had courage; the feet were not placed wide. He was not braced for the grim momento; his feet were almost together, as though he were about to dance. He appeared almost lounging in the street.

Now Josey spoke again, very slow. "Chato," he called softly, not taking his eyes from Morino.

"Si," Chato answered from the building shadow.

"Tell Mr. Pancho Morino that seeing as how he's sich a good feller, sich as thet, I'll leave it to him to call the turn. He can pitch his hat in the air, anytime he gits to feeling thataway. When it touches the ground, we let 'er rip. Remindst him, howsoever, 'bout our hoss trade."

The fluid Spanish of Chato was the only sound; somewhere, someone creaked a door to watch. Morino did not take his eyes from Josey as Chato talked, but he flashed a quick smile. Making a short mocking bow, he said, "Gracias, Señor Wales. I accept."

Now they stood, Morino smoking his cigar. The minute ticked into two. Morino often delayed his killings. It worked the nerves of his opponent, made him unsure, made him think of the death facing him. But he detected no twitch in the languid appearance of the man before him; he was slightly slouched, true, but no movement of the black vicious eyes that stared into his own, no shifting of the feet; only a slow, calculating chewing of the jaws, measured, deliberate slowness of one who, vastly experienced as a professional executioner, might while away his time absently, waiting for the routine to begin. For the first time in his career as a pistolero, Pancho Morino began to feel the chill creep up his spine. A tremor touched the hand he lifted to his cigar. His mind began to race, to search for the last-minute edge; for now he knew if ever he would need the edge, it would be against this man.

As he smoked, he calculated. The gringo expects me to toss my sombrero up in the air. To offer, to casually give me the right of beginning the reach for the pistola. The man is a fool, or a pistolero of extreme confidence. But consider, if the sombrero is *skimmed* at him, waist-high, it will confuse. Quien sabe? Who knows? He shrugged to loosen the unfamiliar tightening of his nerves. In the confusion, the gringo's hand might jerk. Perhaps he could not see the hand of Pancho Morino. He dropped the cigar.

Still the scar-faced pistolero before him did not move, did not even cease the irritating rhythm of the chewing jaws. Slowly Pancho Morino lifted his left hand to his sombrero. His fingers clutched the brim. Suddenly he jerked it, skimming the hat toward Josey.

But when he jerked, the sun hit him square in the eyes. The figure before him dimmed and he hesitated to clear his sight. The edge was lost. The hat sailed, tilted and plunged. As it flicked the dust, Pancho Morino's hand quicksilvered to push the handle of his pistola; tilting the holster, he got off his shot; but the gringo had moved a full step to Pancho's right!

Like fluid lightning he moved. The puffs ballooned from his barrel.

Pancho Morino felt the hammer blows, one so quick behind the other they were almost one. They knocked him backward into the dust. Pancho knew he had lost. He lay, conscious, staring up at the hot blue sky. How blue it was! There was no pain.

A shadow fell over him. It was Josey Wales. He had holstered his pistol. He had fanned it twice. Josey Wales knew where he hammered home his bullets.

Neither Pablo, Chato, or Morino's men moved a muscle. They stood silent. Josey looked down into the pistolero's eyes.

"Where's Escobedo?" he asked softly.

"Aldamano . . . sixty Rurale trash . . . bestia," Morino whispered. "He waits for my messenger . . . that you are dead. I pray . . . you kill him!"

Life was flowing from him, turning the dust black in the circle, mud beneath his body.

"He have prisoners?" Josey asked.

"Si, uno gringo . . . uno Apache . . ."

He lifted a surprisingly small and delicate hand, fumbling at his jacket. Josey knelt, drew the black cigar and sulphur matches. He struck the match on Morino's silver buckle and lit the cigar. Slowly he placed it between the bandido's lips and stood erect.

"Gracias," Morino whispered. "My horse . . . is yours . . . my guns . . ."

"I'll take the hoss; it was a trade," Josey said, "but I don't take from the body of sich as you."

"Then we share . . . something . . . even in this . . . compadres." Morino's whisper was weakening. "My men are coming. When they see you with the horse . . . they will know who won the game of death. They will let you pass . . . it . . . is . . . my honor."

"Reckin," said Josey, "that's all as sich as you and me has got, thet we can take with us. Adios." He turned to go, his shadow passing from the body of Pancho Morino.

"I was fast . . . eh?" Morino's whisper followed him.

"You was fast," said Josey Wales, and walked away.

Pancho Morino tried to smoke the cigar, it was good; but the life fled quickly. It dropped from his lips and burned a hole in his silvered jacket.

They took the big dapple horse. Chato led it behind Josey as they rode west, past the church. Behind them the two bandidos knelt, hats off, beside their fallen leader.

The Priest stood on the steps of his church. His thin face showed nothing as they passed. He crossed himself and was surprised as the bandido following the scar-faced one doffed his sombrero politely, and the one-armed Indian bandido crossed himself in a pious manner, even managing to pull his sombrero from his head in the passing.

The scar-faced bandido appeared not to notice the Priest. He spat filthy tobacco in the street and seemed to be looking upward at the top of the church. Perhaps he is looking heavenward, thought the Priest, in fear of his lost soul.

But of course, the Priest did not know the way of Josey Wales.

10

They galloped west, into the sun. Hangings usually take place at dawn, in the mind of Josey Wales, who had seen many. He'd heard that Ten Spot's would come in the morning, at Aldamano.

For ten miles they set a fast gait, raising the powdery dust behind them, until they saw the first two sentinels.

They sat their horses by the roadside, one to a side; then further on, two more. Josey dropped the horses to slow jog, and looking neither right nor left, rode steadily between them.

Chato, leading the big horse of Pancho Morino, followed. Pablo in the rear. It was like a gauntlet. No word was said. But as they passed, each pair of bandidos lifted their huge sombreros and held them to their chests.

Pancho Morino was dead. He had died in combat of honor; else his killer would not have lived past the guns of Morino's back-up men in Coyamo.

Pablo shyly tipped his sombrero to each in the passing. Chato rode with the proud dauntlessness of the vaquero, roweling his horse and reining him down, to sidle and prance, stepping high by the bandidos. Josey Wales rode casually, almost sidesaddle; his weight on one stirrup, half turned as though resting in the saddle—but his side vision brought in the rear.

The wind mourning in the sage, the slow clip-clop of the horses were the only sounds. Two, four, six, a dozen, sixteen, twenty bandidos sat silently on horseback at their passing.

A hundred yards beyond the last two sentinels, Josey pulled up. They turned to watch. The bandidos were riding hard for Coyamo. The merest hint of sweat rolled down the nose of Josey Wales. He plug-cut the tobacco and chewed as he watched them disappearing in the dust cloud.

"That un," he opined, "was clost—and you, ye crazy Mex," he jabbed a finger at Chato, "didn't help na'ar bit, a-prancin' and a-paradin' around about the whole god-damned situation."

Chato laughed uproariously. "You no comprendes, Josey. It is the right of victor in combat of honor. It was the pride in my bandido chieftain. The bandidos, they comprendes!"

Pablo shook his head at the disappearing dust cloud. "I would not want to live in Coyamo tonight," he said.

"Nor I," Chato answered. "If I was in Coyamo, I would run."

The trail was before them, flat and straight, stretching

endlessly through the plain. They jerked their hats lower against the sun.

Chato pulled beside the jogging gait of Josey's roan. "I watched you, Josey," he said with prideful awe. "I have not seen the quickness before."

Josey spat at a scurrying horned toad, not allowing enough lead, and so only dirtied its tail. He frowned. "The Lord gives to sich as they can do different things. Pablo to make things grow, and live; me, I reckin, to kill."

If there was the hint of bitterness in his voice, he was thinking of Pancho Morino. That man—with a little more of the Code, what he might have become. He hated the thought of Coyamo.

"Why did you move to your left, like the fast water flows, as you drew the pistola?" Chato asked curiously.

The horses, jogging, covered a quarter mile before Josey answered.

"Well," he drawled, "that there swivel gun was tight agin' his hip—had to be, to kick 'er up straight fer his shot; which is fine fer close quarters, saloons and sich, but he couldn't turn it fer 'nough right, at my distance, I figgered. Which he couldn't."

They rode awhile in silence. Then: " 'Course, the sun helped a mite."

"The sun?" Chato asked, surprised.

"Why shore," Josey said, "thet was the reason fer the extry hour—put the sun behind me; thet and allowing Pancho a little more liquoring time."

"Hola!" came from Chato.

"Ain't nothing special 'bout thet," said Josey. "Every town marshal in the west, which has lived long enough, knows. Ye've heerd tell. When a boar coon comes ripping into town, liquoring and shooting and sich, the marshal sends him word to git out of town by sundown, er meet him in the street. 'Course, the marshal makes damn shore he's at the west end, with the sun behint his back—and the ol' boar coon, he's done liquored hisself up proper. Thet is to say, sich is the practice of town marshals which has lived the longest. Gittin' a little edge ofttimes stretches out his living by 'most a year er two."

"There is more," Chato said solemnly, "to being a pistolero than quickness of the hand."

"Ye could say thet, I reckin, fer them that lives longer. Which ain't exactly to set in a rocking chair, howsoever," Josey added drily. "Anyway ye look at it, it ain't much of a trade to take up, saying a feller has a choicet."

"Why the horse?" came from Pablo, who had pulled up on Josey's right. "Why must we have Señor Morino's horse?"

"Thet hoss," answered Josey, "is the onliest one I've seed thet can stay with ourn on a chase."

"On a chase?" Pablo was bewildered.

"Yep, thet's Ten Spot's hoss. We're going to git right popular when we yank Ten Spot out'n that hoosegaw tonight."

It was a thought to bring silence as they rode into the huge red ball of the setting sun, toward Aldamano, Capitan Jesus Escobedo and sixty Rurales.

For Pablo, it was a thought bringing stoic resignation to suicide. And so this way he was to die.

For Chato Olivares, the thought raced reckless excitement through his body, exulting at the prospect, wild as the plains winds.

For Josey Wales, it was the thought of the guerrilla, veteran of two hundred fights on the Missouri-Kansas border. And the thoughts of the guerrilla are the double-think: How was the other feller thinking? What was his plan? His character? What did he expect? Necessary thoughts for a guerrilla; for his was the life of the counter-punch, flexible, unorthodox, too small of force to initiate campaigns; and so for him the war was the war of the mind. He must do the unexpected, unexpected by his enemy; or he was dead.

Night swept away the purpling dusk of the plain and brought the stars, among them the Indian-bow sliver of new moon; beginning of the Comanche moon, they called it.

In the winter, the Comanche struck, lightning fast on horseback, deep into Mexico; but in the spring, they rode away to the north, a thousand, two thousand miles, like the wind storming over the plains. Leaving the quietude of finished havoc in its path. But at least there was the respite from Comanche in the spring and summer. The Apache never left.

The Apache was always there. With each birth of morning, in the purple of dusk, in the black of night. The Apache.

An hour into the night, they saw Aldamano. First, a pinprick of flickering light. As they came closer, the lights were brighter, glowing the sky. Aldamano kept the torches burning all night, every night; for looming high, dark and foreboding, close to her western skirts of Spanish civilization, were the Sierra Madre.

As they drew closer to the town, Josey slowed the horses to a walk. They rode single-file on the very edge of the trail, where the soft churned dust muffled sound, where the mesquite waved in the wind at their heads, making them a part of the undulating landscape.

Two miles from Aldamano they stopped; fifteen, thirty minutes they sat their horses, and Josey uttered no word. He kept the long-glass to his eye, sweeping around first one side, then the other of the town.

He clucked the roan into motion. "Ain't no outriders," was his only comment. They walked the horses steadily onward toward the town. Closer; the lighted town loomed larger.

Bringing up the rear, Pablo prepared himself for death. By the Santos! Were they going to ride into the town, down the main street? Sixty savage Rurales!

A half mile from town, Josey led them off the trail into thick bushes. "Grain the hosses with nose bags," he said softly.

"But we grained them not long ago, Josey . . . ," Chato began.

"I know," Josey said, his voice a snarling whisper, "but nose bags stops hosses from snorting and whinneying their damn noses when they smell some more hosses. Which in about half a minute they's going to do, if ye don't move pronto!" The nose bags went on—pronto!

They sat in a tight circle of darkness. The wind rustled the mesquite and sage, and brought sounds of music, laughter and loud voices from the town.

"A fiesta," Chato said longingly. Josey chewed meditatively, listening for more portent sounds.

"Way I figger," he said finally, "Escobedo picked the wrong man, fer him, when he picked Pancho Morino. I could be wrong. But I ain't. Them kind of fellers—Escobedo—thinks anybody Morino's class ain't got no code, no pride, sich. He figgered Morino to jest set up a bushwhack with twenty guns and chop us down."

"This I also believe," Chato said. "He could have found plenty such men, but he believe a peon, a peon bandido is a bestia. Pancho Morino take—took pride in his pistolero reputation—an hombre mucho."

"I also believe this," Pablo said, though he had no idea as to where the "figgerin' " was leading.

"Figgerin' thisaway . . . ," Josey paused, "which is right, because Mr. Escobedo couldn't never believe he was wrong about peons, Indians and sich, it would shake his guts out;

then he'll believe every word of it, when the messenger from Morino tells him Josey Wales is dead. Ain't no other way he can believe. Proves he was right."

"The messenger?" Chato was surprised.

"Yeah," Josey said casually. "Morino told me Escobedo was waiting on him to send a messenger that I was dead."

"Hola!" Chato exclaimed. Then: "But who can we send to . . ." His voice trailed off in the wind.

"Now figgerin' on along," Josey mused, ignoring Chato's question, "Escobedo being, like you said, a politician, he's trying to make hisself a big coon in the holler. He'll double back on Morino's men, chop 'em up. Make hisself might near the biggest boar coon this here part of Mexico. Stands to reason." He chewed slower. "Wonder how many Rurales that'll bring out of Aldamano? Have to be right smart. Morino's got twenty guns . . ." This last he voiced almost to himself, so that Chato and Pablo bent close to listen.

"I am the messenger!" Chato leaped to his feet.

"Right as rain; so ye be," drawled Josey Wales. "Ain't none of 'em seed ye. Onliest thing worries me is yer brain."

"What you mean, my brain?" Chato was indignant. He stood up, hitched his pistol belt and moved to his horse.

"See what I mean?" Josey said. "Ye're ready to stick yer haid in a snake pit and ain't even figgered how to count the snakes. Set down." Chato squatted, excitement dancing in his eyes.

"Fust off, ye ride Morino's horse; thet's proof ye're from Morino. Ye're his lieutenant—some sich Mex name —use yer own. Second. *Try* to act like ye're a little skittish about the whole thing. Third. Look and see where is the jail and how many guards they got around it; how it sets and sich. Fourth. When ye come out'n meeting Escobedo, ye ride *fast* and git out of town pronto!" Josey chewed slowly and thoughtfully for a while. Chato shuffled his feet in irritation, anxious to be gone.

"Reckin ye can git all that crowded in ye haid, without'n it running out'n yer ears?"

"Si, si!" Chato said impatiently. He swung aboard the big dapple horse of Morino's and ran his fingers over the silver-trimmed saddle. "What a saddle!" he exclaimed. "When we get back home, Josey, I will trade for the saddle a . . ."

"Godalmighty!" Josey spat disgustedly. He came close to the mounted Chato, reached up and grabbed his arm, hard.

"Not many men could do it, compadre," he said with steel-softness. "Be careful—Escobedo is a snake thet can see . . ."

The words of the outlaw brought moisture in the eyes of the emotional Chato; beneath the hardness of Josey Wales, Chato knew he was full of care. It meant much to be of brotherhood to such a man.

"Vaya con Dios!" Pablo whispered.

Chato jerked the rein, whirling his horse on back feet, hiding his quick emotion, and galloped down the trail toward the lights and the noise, the streets of Aldamano. In the distance, he lifted his sombrero in jaunty farewell. He did not look back.

Propped on elbows, Josey sprawled full-length on the trail, the long-glass to his eye. Pablo lay beside him.

He watched Chato gallop his horse almost to the open gates of the town and drop to a slow strot. He grunted in satisfaction—Chato made it 'pear like he was a little skittish.

The big torches flickered their lights over Chato as he jogged down the main street. Josey saw him fling up a hand, waving at someone. A woman ran into the street and Chato stopped.

"By God!" Josey breathed, "ye crazy Mex—now he's—godalmighty! He grabbed her—sonofabitch!"

Pablo began a silent prayer for Chato Olivares: that the Santos would bring reason to his thoughts, that God would intervene in his mind, that . . .

When Chato reached the gates of Aldamano, there was indeed a fiesta; unofficial perhaps, but nevertheless, a celebration.

Aldamano had little occasion to celebrate; three times in the last month, Apache had struck in the night, stealing many horses and mules, killing a dozen guardias.

Aldamano lived tense in its dying, hanging on to life like an old man withering past his allotted time. Sixty Rurales in Aldamano! She was letting down her hair.

The better families, if there were any, were not on the street. The peons had disappeared into their hovels. Rurales rolled from the cantinas waving bottles in the air, fondling the tetas of the cantina girls. Laying them openly in the alleys.

True, guardias were about to discipline their actions; no shooting, no rape, strict orders of Capitan Escobedo—but Aldamano was having a fiesta!

Excitement sparkled the eyes of Chato Olivares. The good times! He waved to a cantina girl and she ran drunkenly toward this handsome bandido with the silver saddle and horse grande.

Chato stopped and she ran her hands up his leg. Such temptation! The words of Josey came back to him—keep his head, eh? He asked the girl for the location of the headquarters policia. She pointed drunkenly to the end of the street, where a low 'dobe sprawled, ramada-fronted. The carcel? the jail? he asked politely. She waved to a long building set deep in the ground. It adjoined the headquarters policia.

"Gracias, señorita!" Chato flashed a smile. He could not

resist bending from the saddle and patting her rounded rump. This Josey saw. Ah! the discipline required to be a bandido! It was enough to break the soul of a man! Perhaps this is why bandidos are so mean, so malo!

He moved the horse forward. The cantina girl ran after him pleading, then cursing him as he left her behind. He waved back to her. Veering his horse, he dodged two Rurales staggering across the street. Matted hair, filthy clothes. They stank as bestias. It was a long street.

Reaching the building, he dismounted slowly, flipping the reins around the hitch rack. As he did, he looked back. Yes, it was a very long street!

Jauntily walking beneath the roof of the ramada, he stepped onto the porch. Lieutenant Valdez stood beside the door, and with him, a bearded sergeant. Chato did not wait for their challenge. With flippant grandeur, he remarked arrogantly, "I come from mi Capitan, Pancho Morino."

Lieutenant Valdez snapped to attention. With only a light tap, and waiting for no answer, he flung open the door, motioning Chato to enter. He was anxiously awaited, without doubt!

Chato stepped into the room and came face to face with Capitan Jesus Escobedo. Escobedo had risen, his thin face tense and drawn. Chato needed to act no part in facing Escobedo. He sensed and saw the cruelty; it smelled, stank, emanating from the man like the odor of excremento— but wrapped in silk.

Two candles lit the low-ceilinged room and made shadows across the face of Chato. He did not remove his sombrero. His eyes narrowed with cruelty and arrogance. He was the living figure of the crazy bandido who flirts with El Muerte.

"Well!" Escobedo snapped nervously, then forced a thin smile. "Welcome, amigo! And the news?"

FORREST CARTER

Chato took his time. Valdez stood behind him, and he glanced backward over his shoulder. Impatiently Escobedo motioned Valdez to leave the room.

With the closing of the door, Chato looked coolly into the eyes of Escobedo. "I am Lieutenant Olivares," he announced proudly. "Mi Capitan Pancho Morino send me on *his* horse as faith of his word. Comprendes?"

"Si, SI!" Escobedo's voice strained in his effort at composure before this arrogant bandido.

"It is done," Chato said nonchalantly, brushing dust from his jacket.

"Done? You say done? Josey Wales is dead? Is this what you mean? Say what you mean, hombre—eh, Lieutenant!"

"Si," Chato said, "Josey Wales is dead, he and his two compadres. When you come, forty-eight hours from this moment—you gave your word, eh?—you will find them lying in the stables."

"Ahhhhhhhh!" Escobedo could not contain himself. He rushed from behind the desk and, placing his hands on Chato's shoulders, held him proudly. "And how?" he asked, "how was it done?"

Chato moved away from the hands. He looked around the room. Snapping his fingers, he said, "Es nada. Twenty rifles from the brush. The work of un momento." He remarked meaningfully, "It has been very dusty on the trail from Coyamo."

"Si, si!" Escobedo rushed behind his desk, pulled two bottles of tequila from a drawer and set them before Chato.

"Perdone, por favor," he said more softly, his eyes growing cat-like, losing the blush of excitement. "A drink to bind our word; take the tequila to your Capitan as a token of my fidelity." He uncorked one of the bottles.

Chato turned it up and drank long. Taking it from his mouth, he wiped his lips. "Hola!" he exclaimed with genuine appreciation, "es tequila buena!"

"Si," said Escobedo, his voice smoother now, more condescending, "from Ciudad de Mexico itself it comes."

Chato corked the bottle and smacked his lips with gusto. He greedily picked up both bottles. "For mi Capitan," he explained.

Walking to the door, he turned and his eyes flashed. "The hours are forty-eight? Verdad?"

"True. Forty-eight," answered Escobedo smoothly, "the honor of my word." His mind was already racing ahead.

With a bottle in each hand, Chato kicked the door. It swung open and he swaggered to his horse. Carefully he placed a bottle of tequila in each saddlebag.

"Buenas noches!" he sang out, but the Capitan had already called Valdez and the Sergeant inside. Chato shrugged.

They did not see him casually swing his mount in the half circle by the jail. One guardia walking, stopping to lean against the low building. Another at the end, by the door, in half shadows. A low four-foot wall ran directly behind the jail.

As he rode by, Chato whistled. It was a peculiar whistle, repeated over and over. The Rurale at the wall raised a hand in halfhearted salute. The crazy rider was whistling a greeting, no doubt drunk. He had never heard such a whistle before.

But deep in the dungeon, tied hand and foot, Ten Spot heard, the peculiar whipping call of the mountain whippoorwill. He knew it well from the mountains of Virginia, and Tennessee.

The last place he had heard it was a place called the Crooked River Ranch, the home of Josey Wales. He stiffened and listened hungrily to the sound growing fainter. An unexplainable thrill ran through his body. In the darkness he puzzled in disbelief. Then he smiled.

Chato jogged down the street. The tequila had warmed him and lifted his optimism. There was nothing to it! He even debated pausing and having another drink from the bottle; but no, it could lead him to abandon his judgment, to visit a cantina. Halfway down the street, three-quarters.

He did not see the door of the headquarters policia open behind him. Escobedo, Valdez and the Sergeant stepped out. Escobedo motioned, and the Sergeant raised the rifle, bracing it against a post of the ramada. He took long, long aim . . . CRACK! The rifle split the air with a lightning jolt.

The hammer hit him hard in the back and Chato reeled. Only a life in the saddle, his superb horsemanship, saved him from falling. Without thought, only instinct to guide him, he loosened the reins as his roweled spurs dug the horse's flanks. His hands gripped the saddle horn.

The big horse leaped instantly in a dead run. More rifles cracked. But Chato Olivares, rolling crazily in the saddle, was riding a horse on a death run. They missed.

Josey Wales was watching. He saw Chato slump, the horse leap, long before the rifle crack reached him. He jumped to his feet. "Bring the hosses," he shouted at Pablo.

Snatching the nose bag from the big roan, he hit the saddle, Indian-style, already running.

He did not head the roan for Chato, but away from him, down the trail toward Coyamo. The roan had to match the speed of the big dapple for him to bring it down.

"Git, Red!" he snarled viciously, and the big horse laid back his ears. He sprang like a puma and bellied out, powerful haunches putting him in a frothing dead heat in ten seconds.

The roan could hear the hoofbeats behind him. He had heard them many times before; they were to be outdistanced. His neck straightened out like a deer's. From his great chest, and his heart, he gave all he had.

There was a horse race—but the roan won it. He matched, then surpassed the dapple's speed, until Josey was forced to pull back on the reins, the roan snorting and protesting, until the dapple could catch up. When the teetering Chato came alongside, Josey leaned and snatched the reins, pulling down the two horses, prancing, snorting and heaving. He rode them fifty yards into a clump of thick mesquite and tied them, still stomping, to the branches.

Chato's head was slumped forward, his sombrero dragging the neck of the horse. Blood pumped from his chest and over the saddle. The heart of Josey Wales froze and tightened his breath. He pulled Chato from the horse, yanking at the iron-gripped hands on the saddle horn, and laid the vaquero on his back.

Quickly he pulled away the shirt. The hole was in the lower chest. He turned him on his stomach and struck a sulphur match. The bullet had missed the spine by a half inch.

Pablo came up with the horses. He saw the blood and ran into the bushes. In a moment he returned, his one arm filled with leaves. "These," he panted, "will stop the blood. They will heal."

While Pablo made a mound of leaves on the back wound, Josey jerked a shirt from a saddlebag. He tore it into strips, and he and Pablo turned Chato, mounding the leaves on the chest, pressing until slowly the blood clotted and stopped.

Josey wound the strips of shirt tightly about Chato, rolling him gently on the ground, and tied the wide bandage with hard twisted knots.

Chato opened his eyes. He smiled weakly in the dim light.

"Es malo . . . bad, eh?" he asked calmly.

"It's bad," Josey said. He struck another match. "Cough and spit in my hand."

Chato made a weak effort. "It hurt to cough, Josey," he protested.

"Cough, damn ye, and spit in my hand," Josey commanded. Chato coughed and spat. By the flickering light, Josey examined the spittle. "Ain't no blood, don't believe yer lung-hit."

"Ah . . . ," Chato breathed, "es bueno. I have always said my luck . . ."

"Yer luck," Josey snarled, "ain't wuth a damn. It could be belly er gut; howsoever," he mused, "it missed yer spine."

"God will save you, Chato," Pablo whispered soothingly, "God will not let you die."

They heard it then, sounding first like faraway thunder. Josey knew the sound.

"I'm moving to the trail," he said softly. "If ye hear gunfire, Pablo, ye git Chato on thet horse somehow er 'nother and ride north."

"I will not ride," Chato said stubbornly. "I can shoot good from here."

"I will stay with Chato," Pablo whispered.

Josey Wales glided away from them, silent as a puma in the brush, and back to them floated his whisper, "Ye stupid bastards!"

He lay by the trail under a bush and watched them pass, galloping in columns of twos. Five, ten, fifteen, twenty, they rode toward Coyamo. Twenty times two reckined out to be forty Rurales!

Silently he slipped back and gave the news to Pablo,

squatting by the side of the sprawling Chato. Chato grinned at the number. Forty Rurales riding out of Aldamano!

"I have done my job bueno, eh, Josey?" he asked, weak but boastful.

"I reckin," Josey answered, "thet is, if ye live."

"Live or die, por Dios!" Chato argued in a whisper, "I have done my job well . . . Remember, Josey, next time there is the need I must borrow ahead of the wages, eh?"

"ALL RIGHT!" snarled Josey Wales, "ye're always reminding me about yer damn borrering."

Chato tried to laugh, but the numbness was leaving and the pain cut into his breath.

The sliver of moon dropped further to the west. A coyote raised a tenor voice that carried long on the wind. Josey sat close to Chato and Pablo. He cut his tobacco plug and chewed, looking absently into the waving, wind-whipped mesquite.

"Well?" Chato gasped. The pain was telling. "Is it not now the time to get Ten Spot . . . while the Rurales are gone?" The pain and Josey's unconcerned, methodical chewing made Chato irritable. After all this, were they to sit here like cows?

After a long time, Josey answered, "Figger at the best— thet is, pushing them hosses might near dead—best them Rurales can do is five hours to Coyamo."

"But," Pablo suggested quietly, "if we got Señor Ten Spot now, it would give us many more hours start."

"Reckin not," Josey said. He looked at the moon. "Ye see them military kind of fellers don't never learn. They always change guards at midnight. Saying we went and got Ten Spot now—time I got there and sich, they'd find them dead guards in jest about thirty minute when they come to change their midnight shift. Nope," he chewed thoughtfully, "we'll wait till after midnight; there's yer four-, maybe six-hour start; dependence on how long their guard duty runs, less'n we're unlucky and somebody discovers them dead guards by accident."

"Dead guards?" Pablo asked, bewildered at the "figgerin'."

"Well," Josey said, "it'll either be one way or t'other. I could jest stop by, tip my hat and say as we have come fer Mr. Ten Spot, and would they please turn him loose. But, more'n likely, throat cutting will git the job done. We do the cutting, er they do, take yer pick."

"How will you know . . . the time?" Chato asked weakly.

"I'll know," Josey answered. He lay back on the ground and watched the moon sliver edge downward. After a moment, he lazily called, "Pablo."

"Sí?"

"Git some jerky beef from a bag and let thet dribbling loudmouth Chato chew on it. When he swallers, we'll know if he's belly-shot."

Pablo got the beef and handed it to Chato, placing a rolled blanket under his head, and wondered at the mysteries of the mind, and ways of Josey Wales.

11

When Chato fell forward at the rifle shot, Escobedo clapped his hands in delight. Dead center. There was no doubt. No, no need to chase the rider. Coyamo was not the horse's home. He would run two, three miles and stop to wander and graze the grass.

The shooting had brought Rurales running from the cantinas into the street. While he had their attention, Escobedo shouted, "To the stables! Alert!"

Whirling back into his room, he motioned Valdez and the Sergeant to follow. "Ahora! Now! This you must do. First you, Lieutenant; pick forty of your best men with the rifle. Ride to Coyamo as fast as the horses can stand. Send twenty into the town shooting every bandido on sight. With the additional twenty, encircle the town. Shoot all who run, and those who surrender. No one, NO ONE! of them must live. Comprendes?"

"Si, Capitan," Valdez snapped.

"Most especial, Pancho Morino must die! Assign five of your best riflemen to concentrate. You know his dress. Get Morino!"

"Si! It's done!" Valdez responded vehemently.

"And when you find the Alcalde, who will be hiding beneath his bed no doubt," Escobedo sneered, "tell him our ever vigilant scouts reported to me the movement of bandidos on his town. That I sent the greater part of my force to rescue Coyamo, leaving a small number for me to fight the Apache. Comprendes?"

"Si, Capitan!"

"This," Escobedo placed his hands on the shoulders of Valdez in a grand manner, "will bring much glory to you. Perhaps a promotion to Capitan!"

The eyes of Valdez shone with the eagerness of a blood-wolf. Capitan Valdez! The words rolled around beneath his breath. His chest rose in pride. He snapped to attention and saluted.

"VAMOS!" Escobedo said, and then softly, "Vaya con Dios."

"Gracias, Capitan," Valdez said. He was on a mission of God, and of course, with it came glory as it should. He rushed through the door.

Escobedo had used the genius of approach to Valdez, first, the promise of glory and promotion; second, softly, the feeling of holy mission. He would not fail.

Already, outside he could hear the crisp shouted orders of Valdez, the running feet, the mounting of horses, the thunder of hoofs as the men swept down the street of Aldamano and faded eastward.

Now he turned to the Sergeant. It required effort, but

he allowed the merest hint of benevolent smile to touch his lips. He considered the bearded brutal features, the matted hair stringing beneath the sombrero. A bestia.

"Sergeant, we are bringing our district into order. We will be recognized by the Governor! When Lieutenant Valdez becomes Capitan, it leaves the open place. That is for you, Sergeant—Lieutenant!"

The low brows of the Sergeant lifted. His grin showed yellow teeth. "Si! Mi Capitan!"

"Now!" Escobedo continued, "you are left with a small force; counting yourself, only nineteen men. I place the safety of Aldamano in your hands. Only five may sleep at each time. The others on guard of four hours. Comprendes?"

"Comprendo, Capitan. It's done!" He saluted and moved to the door.

"And Sergeant," Escobedo called, consulting his time-piece, "it is a little past nine. Go to the hacienda of the Alcalde. Inform him as to the mission of Valdez and his troops. Assure him of our vigilance. Tell him I will dine with him and his family at eleven. Comprendes?"

"Si, Capitan. And El Padre? I must tell him also?"

Escobedo frowned. "Noooo, let us leave the Padre to his peace."

The Sergeant left hastily, filled with the importance of his responsibility. Escobedo opened the door and watched him in the torchlight, rushing on his way to the Alcalde, snapping orders to his men as he strode with the swagger of a general on parade.

Ah! one needed only to understand. That is why Capitan Escobedo got the most from his men. His poor, simple-minded Rurales!

No, he thought, as he closed the door and sat down at his desk, he did not want the Padre despoiling, this time, his plan-making with the Alcalde.

When he had first come into Aldamano, he had met with the Alcalde and the Priest. The Alcalde, a broad, puffish politico, had been even more distressed than the Alcalde of Coyamo.

His town was disappearing before him! It was not his fault; after all, so close to the Sierra Madre. What did the Governor expect? Soon, he wailed, there would be nothing here. He would be an innkeeper, a stable peon, left only for service of the passersby hurrying through. All the mines were shut down. There was no activity. He held his hands outward, upward, beseechingly to El Capitan.

Escobedo had listened with the same silent sympathy, nodding his head in agreement, clucking sympathetically.

When the Priest spoke, rage rose in Escobedo's throat. He had seen his kind before, scattered thinly over Mexico.

He was a wizened little man, his face browned by the sun, spent amongst his peons no doubt. He was old, his white hair stringing and unkempt. He began by speaking softly.

"At one time the Governor of Chihuahua made a treaty with the Apache. That our state would pay a few cattle, a few head of mule each year in tribute to the Apache. The Apache came into our towns. He traded. He kept his word; until . . . ," here the Priest paused and his eyes flashed accusingly at the bowed head of the Alcalde, "ambitious, greedy politicos, seeking to crush the Apache, got them drunk on mescal, and while they were drunk, treacherously murdered them. Slaughter, Capitan! Like pigs!"

His voice had risen, and now he paused and stared at the floor of the stone patio. With pathetic hopelessness, he shook his head. "The Apache will trust us no more. He is a guerrilla trained by centuries. He can, and he will, out-match the treachery of ourselves. Which we have earned!"

Escobedo was shocked. "But, Padre . . . !" he began.

"Listen to me!" The little priest rose to his feet.

Escobedo noted with disgust that his robe was poor, tattered. Por Dios! He even wore the barefoot sandal of the peon!

"But un momento," Escobedo interrupted, "why should our government pay tribute to a small group of murderous savages? Where is the sense of it?"

"The sense of it?" the Priest answered, "the sense, Capitan; that it is, or *was*, their land, and we took it. We have exacted tribute in gold and blood from every Indian, from Peru to our northern border, except the Apache. Only the Apache has turned about the process and collected tribute from us. I have seen, Capitan—the priests who demand a peon bring in so many chickens a week, a peso, a bushel of maize; that the peon work without pay in the fields owned by the Church, so many days a week as tribute. I have seen his children work for that tribute. I have seen the whipping posts standing by the Church of God, where the peon has been whipped to death for failing to bring in the tribute of a chicken! The stocks I have seen, into which the peon is yoked to die of thirst!"

The little priest's voice rose in fervor. His eyes burned. "I believe," he continued fervently, "as does our new Presidente, Benito Juarez, the Church should own no land, no mines, no holdings. Only the Church! There should be no tributes, except those given by love!"

"Si! Si!" Escobedo said soothingly, "there is much sense to what El Presidente says, but . . . ," Escobedo shrugged his way from the corner, he could not argue against El Presidente, "I am a man of military, Padre; such things are beyond my authority, my influence. My oath and duty is to Mexico. I am sure you comprendes."

The Priest was obviously mad. Escobedo had no wish to antagonize him, though he was sure he had no influence with the bishops and bureaucracy. It was known he collected nothing from his peons. He contributed no wealth. His poverty made him nada. Escobedo worried little at his ravings.

The Priest was obviously a man who had strayed far from God, concerning himself not with the spiritual, but material things, half paganized by the peon Indians with whom he mingled.

The little priest paced the floor. He placed his hands behind his back. Head down, he walked slowly in thought. He sat down at the table opposite Escobedo. The Alcalde was holding his head in his hands and staring at nothing.

The Priest looked across the candlelight at Escobedo and his eyes softened. "Yes, Capitan, you are a man of military. With your permission, while your Rurales are here, I should like to talk with them, en masse."

The request and soft voice startled Escobedo. "Why, most certainly, Padre. The permission is granted."

"I would like to tell them," the Priest continued, as though Escobedo had not spoken, "of love. I know . . . ," he shook his hand at the acquiescent nod of Escobedo, "that love is only a word to them, and . . . ," he looked piercingly at Escobedo, "to others. But I want to show them it is not just a word. It is a law, when broken, one pays extreme penalty.

"God," he said, "gave man sex, and with it, as with all gifts from God, He gave him a choice in its use. The passion of the sex is only the entry to be used, to open into the great mystery of love. Only the intangible binds, Capitan. The bonds of love, not the physical. And so man has his choice. He may smirk, and joke at this instrument. He can become what he calls the 'sophisticate.' He can encourage, make of his women—his women, who would join him in the mystery of love—objects to be flaunted as animal objects. To make sex a simplification, as of the bowel movement, but . . . ," the Priest pointed his finger at

Escobedo, "as he moves from the sunlight of love, he passes into the twilight of the material, and the twilight does not last long. Soon he finds that his passion will no longer be aroused by the coarseness. He is dissatisfied. He is satiated with the coarseness of nada except sex objects. He cannot remain there, and so then he must pass into the night of sadism, of rape, of terror against others. Here he discovers, once again, the material potency he had lost. But this time it comes from inflicting terror and pain, not in sharing love. He has chosen the opposite—the evil choice always given man, with no satisfaction, only emptiness, never satiated, without end. Rape, Capitan, is not a crime of sex, no more than the knife is a crime of murder. The knife can be used to cut the loaf of bread in the love bosom of the family, or used to plunge terror and death from the sadistic soul of the user. The knife is but the instrument, as is the organ of sex.

"God, giving man a soul, also gives him the choice of rising above the animal with love; but if he disdains it, he cannot remain on the material level of the animal. He cannot stop the degeneration, once he begins. He will inevitably embrace the sadism of El Diablo, and so become lower than the animal. Rapaciousness and violence stalk our land, while we grow more 'sophisticated,' and more 'civilized,' with our coarseness we call 'adult.' The intangible of sadism is El Diablo's answer to God's intangible of love. The rapist is not over-sexed, Capitan, he is under-sexed. His is a lost soul. Losing love, he has lost all. For every blessing God offers man, He also offers him the choice of turning that blessing into a curse!"

The voice of the Padre hardened. His eyes looked accusingly at Escobedo, so that Escobedo was forced to drop his own eyes and examine the tips of his boots.

"The rapes must stop, Capitan," the Priest said, "the violence of terror upon people must cease. Man's soul cannot live in a vacuum without love. It must fill that vacuum. And it will embrace the passion of terror. That . . . ," the Priest rose with finality, "is what I would tell your Rurales, and warn them of their flirtation with laws of which they have no comprehension, in their breaking."

He strode from the patio, seeming taller than his height, more majestic than was reasonable for his tattered robe.

For the brief flicker of an instant, fear entered the heart of Capitan Escobedo; but only for an instant. It was the wine.

The Alcalde had raised his head and looked pleadingly at Escobedo. "You see, Capitan, the cooperation I have from the Padre. My authority is impossible in this position; thus you have witnessed."

"I can see," Escobedo murmured; but with more heart, he encouraged the Alcalde. "If you encourage the growth of my own authority, I shall see that the Padre is removed, perhaps to a pueblo, where he can teach the Indians to make baskets. Perhaps, together, we can raise a city from the ashes!"

"You have the whole of my heart in support," the Alcalde answered enthusiastically. "You are the first hombre I have seen in years to bring hope of growth and civilization."

Escobedo departed. He was uncomfortable. Somehow he felt naked, undressed by the Padre. He had noticed the Padre had offered no blessing on him. Neither had he asked.

Now, as he closed the door behind the Sergeant, he shook the thought of the Padre from his mind. The Padre could be dealt with like all such childish men.

A lone candle lit the room, flickering tiny shadows that grew huge, dancing on the walls.

The two Papago Indian women—he had chosen these

servants, because the Papago hated Apache—had bathed the Apache girl, fed her, cleansed and perfumed her. She had, he considered, almost lost the smell of the Apache animal.

She lay in a corner, bound, face to the wall. Escobedo consulted his watch. His hand trembled: nine-thirty. Plenty of time before eleven.

Seating himself on his bunk, he removed his boots, his shirt, pants and underclothing. So he stood, completely naked, gaining control of the tremors that ran up his body.

He knew the girl was a virgin. He knew because she wore no head band. It was the mark of the Apache. He understood nothing else, for he gave no credence to the Apache as having a code.

In truth, the Apache was very strict, his simple reasoning being that the girl who dishonored herself in playing at the great gift of Usen would, of course, not honor the man she married. It was a code seldom broken, for the Apache girl knew to break the code meant a life without a husband. She would be fed by the band to which she belonged. She could work, yes. She could continue as the plaything of loose men; but she would find no husband. A widow—yes, she could remarry with honor.

Escobedo fathomed no such code among the animals called Apache. Now he walked on bare feet to the corner where she lay. In one hand he held the long knife he had pulled from his belt. He cut away the thongs that bound her feet and pulled her upright by the thong about her neck. She looked up at him, black eyes that burned hate. No fear.

"You are not afraid, querida?" Escobedo whispered hoarsely in Spanish. "Then let us see." He led her into the light of the candle, her hands still tied behind her back.

Slowly with the knife, he began between her breasts, cutting downward, the razor sharpness moving smoothly, separating the buckskin. Downward, until the skirt too fell open.

Savagely, by the neck thong, he jerked her about and ran the knife down the back of her clothing. Her dress fell away and she stood before him, naked.

She was tiny, scarcely five feet; the small, hard tetas pointing up; the flat, firm belly and tight-muscled buttocks. She glowed bronze in the candlelight, black hair falling to her shoulders.

The slightest twitch flicked the muscles of the oval face. Her mind could not control the muscle. Escobedo saw the twitch.

"Ahhhhhhhh! Some doubts, querida? Let us see." Laying the knife on his desk, he bent her backward across it. With his knees he held her legs down, toes touching the floor, and bent her back, pushing her face until she was bowed, arching the spine from the surface of the desk. Only her head and shoulders rested on one edge of the desk; her tiny buttocks pressed the opposite edge.

With one hand, Escobedo held the neck thong, and now with the other, he stroked her arched belly, feeling down for the pubic hair. It had only begun its growth. His breathing was heavier at this confirmation of the tenderness of the untouched girl.

Her legs were pulled tightly together. With one knee, he forced them apart and felt the muscles tremble in her legs. He placed himself carefully at the virgin opening and moved into her—slowly—feeling the tightness, the hard contractions, unfamiliar, foreign to the act.

He watched her eyes intently, but they did not change; no flicker. Suddenly he plunged, throwing himself hard into her, so that he grunted with the effort.

Her body arched higher, belly strained and tightening, bridging the space beneath her. The legs jerked out of control. He pulled outward, and the body came down. He

[122]

plunged again, venomously, and watched the thin body rise in an ecstasy of pain; down—up—still she made no cry, though the legs waved wildly in the air. Still the eyes did not change. Only the body jerked, rising and beating the desk surface. Blood fountained from her. Enough to satiate the most vicious of terrorists; but Escobedo had passed further into the depths of passion by terror. The Priest had sensed—smelled, like Chato—the sadism of the man.

He paused, panting heavily; sweat glistened on his bony body.

He leaned his face close to her small stoic eyes. He was still deep within her; and in slow, clear Spanish, so she would know, he spoke softly. "I am told, querida, that there is a sensation, an exultation, and experience that comes to few men. Do you know what that is, eh? It is the experience of being, as I am now, deep within the virgin. As she dies, the death throes, the contractions, are beyond imagination. Shall we try this experience, little querida?" Madness hoarsened his whisper.

He began to tighten the thong about her throat. Feverishly he watched, as he tightened—tighter—tighter. Her eyes began to bulge. He felt within her a twisting iron that moved in velvet. Her face turned blue. Her tongue popped out. She collapsed.

The passion at last was drained from Escobedo. Her bowels had loosed, flooding him and the desk with excremento. He stepped back, exhausted, disgusted. He was weak as he shoved her from him to the floor, and for only a moment could bear the sight of the wreckage.

He rushed into the washroom behind his office. Cleansing himself, trembling. He dressed in full uniform, careful to polish his boots, flicking the dust from his sleeves.

His legs were weak, and he would not look at the figure on the floor as he passed. Lifting a bottle of tequila, he gulped hungrily. As he opened the door, he consulted his timepiece: ten forty-five. He would be punctual for his appointment with the Alcalde. As he walked down the street, he felt relaxed, warmed by the tequila. Seeing the Sergeant, he stopped him.

"Go to my office, clean up the carnage—of the bestia. Wrap her in blankets. You may hang her outside the western gate of Aldamano, facing the Sierra Madre."

"Si, Capitan," the Sergeant answered impassively. He knew what he would find. He had performed the task many times. He shrugged his brutish shoulders and prepared himself for the stench of the job.

Escobedo, for all his brilliance of maneuver, his cunning in plan, possessed a flaw that cracked the hard solidity of his ambitions. Always, he looked upon those "beneath" him as moronic figures, having no powers of thought, of character, or honor. And like all such men, he never saw the flaw; only cursed the crises that developed, first here, then there, and would of course eventually destroy him.

As the Sergeant had acknowledged to himself, he had performed such an act many times, but never on an Apache.

For an Apache to divine one's thoughts in advance is bad—for the thinker. To tell an Apache one's thoughts is very, very bad. It simplifies the guerrilla art of the double-think.

Escobedo had told the girl in the Spanish she understood. She was to die. He told her how she was to die. He told her what he expected of her at her death.

For generations, the Apache, the guerrilla raised from childhood, accepted the way of riding the thin line between life and death.

Automatically, the girl moved to that line. Not too soon. It would betray the farce. Five seconds before her eyes would have bulged in death, she bulged the eyes. She tensed the neck; and not just before, but within three seconds of death, the tongue shot forward. Inside her, she gave him what he demanded. The pain did not matter. She moved muscle against pain, harder, harder, contracting into a bloody fit, sliding tightening muscles—and so drained the passion from him.

Every Apache was familiar with death, the loosening of the bowels, and so she forced it, disgusting Escobedo. But as he had flung her to the floor, her hand behind her back held the handle of the razor-edge knife, held it in a death grip that would not release.

While Escobedo had washed and cleansed himself, she took bare sips of air, only enough for survival, as she had eaten scraps from the ground on the trail. Discipline against the gulping for life; only enough to hold back the dark line of death.

Now, with the room empty, the knife moved easily through the thongs about her wrists. She reached one hand to her throat and loosened the thong. A huge round welt, blue and thick as a rope, circled her throat and neck. She did not think of it. Her thoughts were on survival and the double-think of the guerrilla. Escobedo would send some one quickly to remove her. She lay back as she was before, hands behind her back.

The Sergeant flung open the door and closed it. He came across the room, around the desk. Seeing the sight, he cursed beneath his breath, "Excremento! Always excremento! I would sooner clean the pens of the hogs." He grumbled to himself as he turned his back on the girl. Taking a blanket, he spread it on the floor and came to drag her onto it.

He bent to grab her hair, close to her face. The hand shot up like the head of a snake. The knife point went home, straight through the throat, so viciously it snapped

the spine at the base of the Sergeant's skull. His brain had
no time to register the event of death. He only looked
blank as he fell over the girl.

Weakly she pushed him from her. She rolled him,
crawling and pushing, under the bunk of Escobedo, hiding
him from sight.

She tried to stand, but her legs buckled. She crawled,
pulling herself up with her hands to the edge of the desk;
she blew out the candle and crawled to the rear door of
Escobedo's quarters.

Now her knees collapsed. She pulled, desperately up, and
lifted the latch, held on as she swung through the door,
pulling it shut behind her.

Her knees would no longer support her weight. With
her elbows she pulled along the wall, past the rear of the
headquarters, along the wall of the jail. It was here that
blackness overcame the tenacious Apache will. She
sprawled unconscious against the jail wall. The knife,
tightly, was in her hand.

12

Josey rose from his sprawling consideration of the moon and walked into the brush. He searched here and there, cutting with his kife the heaviest inside growth of the mesquite. In a few minutes he was back and sat down, whittling away the branches and the limbs.

When he was through, he had four sticks, each about five feet long. "A mite limber. They don't grow nothing down hereabouts like the Tennessee mountain country."

"What are they for?" Pablo asked.

"Figgered I might need some walking canes, whenever I'm walking around Aldamano," he said. Pablo puzzled, but did not ask. Walking canes?

Chato had been sleeping, his breath coming in short

gasps moving his chest spasmodically. He had chewed the jerked beef, as much as he could, and drifted off. Now the pain and talk brought him awake.

"How ye feel?" Josey asked, kneeling by his head. "Does yer belly feel paining?"

"I don't know, Josey," Chato said earnestly, "I am hurt all over, my chest, my belly; even my toenails, they are hurting." He rolled his eyes up. "Josey, before I left Escobedo, by the goodness of his heart, he give two bottle of tequila. One for me. One for Pancho. They are in the saddlebag. Maybe, used as medicine, they would help."

Josey went to the horse and brought back the bottles. One he placed in the saddlebag of Chato's gray horse; the other he uncorked and handed to the vaquero.

"Drink a little o' that firewater, by God. We'll know right quick about yer belly; thet is, if it don't numb ye fust from the head down."

Chato raised the bottle and drank. Weakly he smacked his lips and smiled, "Es bueno, good medicine; already I feel it helps me." He raised the bottle again, held it long before lowering it. "Por Dios! It's amazing. I feel I can fork a horse. I am ready for Aldamano."

Enthusiasm rose in the heart of Chato. "You know, Josey, while I ride out of the town, I see the prettiest little señorita; she—when this is over—we must come back to Aldamano." He laid his head back on the blanket and leered crookedly at the sky. "Si! we must come back!"

"We'll come back," Josey said softly.

"Si," Pablo, kneeling at Chato's head, whispered reassuringly, "we will come back."

"Bueno," Chato whispered. His face showed white in the dimness and lines of pain dragged at his jaws. He looked old.

Josey unbuckled and untied the heavy .44's from about his waist. He hung them on the saddle horn of his horse.

Stooping, he picked up the sticks and gathered the reins of the roan and the dapple.

"I reckin," he remarked casually, "I'd better be gittin' along."

"I too am going," came from Chato. He tried to rise, struggled to his elbows and toppled on his side.

"Lay him back on the blanket, Pablo," Josey said grimly. Pablo, pulling and pushing at Chato's shoulders, laid him down.

"I'll be back directly, with Ten Spot," Josey said, "but jest in case ye hear gunfire—I don't mean one shot from some drunk Rurale, I mean business gunfire, rapid fire—Pablo, ye git thet crazy Mex on his hoss someway, and head direct north. Ye hear?"

"Si, I hear, Josey."

Weakly from his blanket, Chato spoke. "Will not run, Josey . . . if you are chased, you lead them this way. We will ambush . . . we will shoot from the brush . . . we will shoot them down like the dog . . ."

"Me too," Pablo said.

Josey whirled on them venomously. "Listen, goddamn ye; if I git in a fight, I'll git out of it. I ain't concerning myself atall about no dribbling cowhand and one-armed farmer! Ye can lay here and rot fer what I give a damn. Ye understand?"

"Si . . . I understand," Chato whispered.

Josey walked, leading the horses, through the brush and disappeared quickly in the darkness.

"Does he mean what he say?" Pablo asked Chato.

Chato grinned. "Josey Wales mean what he do, not what he say. Josey Wales," he continued, a note of pride creeping into his whisper, "he would stand in front of the stampeding cattle if we lie in their path. He like to say he don't care."

"And you—would so stand?" asked Pablo.

"I would stand," Chato said, and drifted into blissful blackness.

There was no mystery to what Chato and Pablo thought was the uncanny "telling of the time" by night as practiced by Josey Wales. For over eight years in the Border War of Missouri, most of his riding, his "work," had been in the night.

And so like the farmer, working by day, who looks at the sun and tells the time within minutes, so Josey Wales could do with the stars and the moon. He knew the night heavens as well as any sailor, and better, for his purpose. He knew the timing of their movements.

He had time to spare. And so he walked, two miles by his figgerin'. The walk would stretch his legs, put him there in plenty of time, and give the edge of not presenting the silhouette of a rider above the bushy tops of mesquite.

He tied the rope of the dapple to the horn of the roan's saddle. They walked single-file, rather than two abreast. It was better for walking in heavier brush, lessened the width of open space and narrowed their target, approaching a man, to a thin black line.

Such care in the smallest detail was second nature, instinct for Josey Wales. In the beginning, he had learned much of it from his Captain, the daring guerrilla, Bloody Bill Anderson. But his Tennessee mountain cunning had added the finesse that Bloody Bill would have longed to possess.

The night wind lessened to a whisper in the mesquite and sage, faintly whining on the cactus spines and the spears of Spanish dagger. Here and there a snake, night hunting, slithered away in the sand.

Josey approached closer to Aldamano, listening to the sounds, for their rhythm, and watching for the familiarity of the way back by which he must come.

He circled wide to the north, around the wall of

Aldamano. The jail was on the western edge of town; and as he circled, he listened for the town noises. There were not any. Good, if they was sleeping off a drunk. Bad, if they wasn't.

He shrugged his shoulders. After midnight was a good time to hit most anything. Everybody was either drunk, half asleep, or sleeping. It was an edge.

Oncet, he remembered, he had jokingly remarked to Bloody Bill thet he wisht the banks which held the Yankee army payrolls, stayed open till after midnight. It would make it a hell of a lot easier than like they had to do, hit 'em in the open sun with every bushy-tailed boar coon around, wide awake and ready. Bill had said thet when they won, he would make hisself governor and he would pass a special law to make the banks stay open till after midnight. Jest fer Josey Wales. Josey chuckled at the remembering.

He must be gittin' on, to commence rec'lectin' sich. Anyhow, Bill went down with two smoking pistols in his hands before the situation was decided one way or t'other —so it didn't matter.

Now he was on the northwest of the town. He had scanned the wall as he walked. No guards on the wall; scared of 'Pache arrows, more'n likely. He began to slant closer to the town in his walk.

'Peared like the torches was burning a mite lower; more shadows. He couldn't see the street. Now he was directly west. He took a deep breath and closed in. Fifty yards from the wall, he spotted the low-slung jail, as Chato had described it. He tied the horses firmly in mesquite. Hanging his hat on the saddle horn, and bending, he half ran, falling lightly, rising to run again in the crouch. He brought himself up beside the wall.

Not even the keen eyes of Josey Wales had seen them. Several times he passed within three feet of Apache. They let him pass. Any hombre moving as he was on the town of Aldamano meant no good for Aldamano, and so this was good for the Apache.

The wall was only four feet high, white 'dobe. Cautiously he raised his head. He was midway on the wall of the jail. He bent and ran farther. Slowly he raised again. He was at the end. He saw the heavy oak door, the guard leaning against the wall, sombrero tilted over his face. Josey sat down and laid his sticks beside him. It was not yet midnight. He would wait, patient as the Indian.

Somewhere in the town, he could hear faint talking; but it was far away and he could make no sense of it.

After a long time, he heard them. "Buenas noches, compadre." That would be the new guard, full of vinegar. The one answering him mumbled tiredly. "Nada" was all Josey heard. That there, according to Chato, meant "nothing." Josey watched them over the wall, the off-duty guard slouching around the corner of the jail and disappearing. Still he waited.

When a guard first came on duty, he was bushy-tailed and went around guarding like hell; but in a little while, just a little while, monotony was the edge. Josey Wales watched as the guard walked about, kicking at the ground. Once he walked almost to the wall, directly at Josey, but turned and repaced his way to the jail door. Now Josey watched him intently, as a scientist watches a bug.

The guard yawned, leaned against the wall, propping his rifle beside him. Josey picked up the sticks and, silent as a shadow, rolled over the wall and lay there, and watched. Five minutes, ten, he watched. The guard did not move.

Silently Josey picked up two of the sticks and slid the Cherokee knife from his boot top. With the sticks under his armpits, he moved, head down, eyes up, watching the guard, closer. He was within five yards when the guard looked up, startled. "Que esta? What is this?" He looked curiously at the stumbling man, unarmed, supporting himself on sticks, obviously wounded.

He came forward, leaving his rifle, to look at this helpless head-down victim, within a yard, and Josey Wales sprang. The knife went upward under the breastbone, buried to the hilt. With the knife plunge, he shoved his open hand into the guard's astounded mouth. They stood thus a moment, silent statues.

The horror in the eyes of the Rurale, staring back at him the vicious eyes of Josey Wales. He died, slumping into Josey without a sound.

Grunting lightly, Josey pushed him to the wall by the door. Using the sticks, he placed one under the pit of each arm and propped the guard against the wall.

Now he crawled in the shadows of the jail. At the corner he could see the main street. There was no one in sight. The Rurales were placing their heaviest guards around the horses and mules, notorious prizes for thieving Apache.

Halfway down the jail wall, he saw the other guard, leaning against the wall. He was about to move on him in the same manner, when his roving eye picked up the figure and he froze.

A Rurale stationed on a rooftop, still as a post, vigilant. Josey began to scan the roofs and saw another farther down the street. He sat back in the shadows. When he got Ten Spot out, time was what he needed—had to have. The guard down the wall was bound to walk up, at anytime, and then raise the alarm. That there guard had to be got—but how? He cut a plug of tobacco with the bloody knife and chewed slowly, squatting in the shadows, meditating the whole damn situation.

"Well," he muttered after an appropriate time of chewing, " 'pears I done fancied out on tricks. Onliest way looks like the simplest."

He rose from his haunches. Yanking the sombrero from the head of the dead guard, he pulled it low over his forehead and eased his head around the corner.

Now, he mused to himself, what, er how, am I a-goin' to call the sonofabitch. I cain't jest say, c'mere, sonofabitch. He remembered the casual, careless Chato; and so, easing his head around the corner, he said, low, "Eh?" and lazily waved his arm, gesturing the guard to him.

The "eh" so casual, the arm lazy, it was obviously no emergency. The guard did not even bring his rifle. He sauntered up the wall. When he reached the corner, Josey Wales simply reached around him with the knife and slit his throat, so deep and brutal the head almost flipped from the neck.

He dragged him beside the door, with the other dead Rurale. Quickly he went through their pockets. There was no key. He felt around them; on the back of the guard propped against the wall, he found the key fastened to his belt. He jerked the key free.

It was a huge key, rusted, and as he turned it in the lock it screeched, opening the door.

The musty smell of damp earth and rotting straw hit his face. He stepped downward on the stone. There was no sound. He chanced a whisper. "Ten Spot! Air ye there?"

From the darkness along the far wall a weak chuckle of laughter answered. "I'm right here, Josey." Josey ran across the straw and found him, hands bound behind his back, feet tied.

He ran the knife through the thongs. "How'd ye know it was me?" he asked the gambler.

Ten Spot answered wryly, "Well, when you asked the question, I said to myself: now Ten Spot, that is a very peculiar Tennessee mountain way of talking for a Rurale, I said; only one fool I know would come . . ."

"Shet up," Josey growled, "we got to git."

As Josey helped him to his feet, Ten Spot stumbled and fell. Josey dragged him up against the wall and carried him to the door. He stopped, looking out cautiously.

"I believe I can stand," Ten Spot whispered.

Gingerly Josey stood him against the wall. He held on for a moment, then turned loose. Ten Spot stood. He watched as Josey brought two more sticks and propped the second dead guard against the wall. He was working quickly, making no sound, except to snarl at Ten Spot, "Make yerself some use; take them pistol belts and pistols off'n them guards. We'll more'n likely have need of 'em."

Ten Spot staggered up to the guards. He shuddered; the throat-cut guard's neck looked like a monstrous mouth. It was smiling broadly and slavering blood. He forced himself to unbuckle the heavy pistol belt, holding the holstered pistol.

Josey stripped the belt from the second guard. "Let's move," he said, and holding Ten Spot by the arm, they moved for the wall. It was then they saw the Apache girl.

Josey dropped to his knees. She was naked, blood-smeared. He felt her heart. "She's alive."

Ten Spot looked down at her. "She was a prisoner too. Escobedo had done this to her. I don't know how she got here."

Josey Wales hesitated for the barest moment; he bent, picking up the girl and slinging her over his shoulder. He pushed Ten Spot toward the low wall. He had to help the gambler get over, surprised at his weakness and skeletal frame. Then he followed with the girl.

They ran for the bushes. Josey laid the girl across his saddle, pushed Ten Spot onto the back of the dapple horse. He jumped astride the roan, but they did not run. Slowly they walked the horses into the shadows of the waving mesquite, away from Aldamano.

Josey guided them, never increasing the pace, through

the winding bushes. Ten Spot reeled in the saddle; black matted beard covered his face, almost a skeleton face. He still wore the black frock coat, but he had no shirt.

Josey whistled, and was answered by Pablo. As they rode into the little circle, Josey motioned for Pablo to take the girl. "The leavings of Capitan Escobedo," was his only explanation.

He eased her down. With his one arm, Pablo tenderly laid her on a blanket. He covered her naked body with another blanket. Josey helped Ten Spot from the saddle, and the gambler sat down suddenly. He looked at Chato, still asleep. "What's the matter with Chato?" he asked.

"Back-shot by Escobedo," Josey said. He stood for a long moment, hat pushed back from the scarred face. "Damned if we ain't set up a horspital, right out here in the middle of nowheres." It was the typical reaction of Josey Wales to disaster.

He was no fool. He knew there was no humor in it. Deep in the heart of enemy territory, riders would be coming, good riders from the east and from the west. Riders who knew the country. Riders who would kill.

The band of Josey Wales was made up of the farmer Pablo, the gambler Ten Spot, Chato badly wounded, and the Apache girl. It was not a band put together for speed in outdistancing pursuers. The odds in a fight would not attract the most reckless of gamblers.

But Josey Wales had learned his guerrilla warfare in the Border War; disastrous situations came as regularly as dinnertime; no quarter asked, no quarter given. He had also learned that the leader lifted those who followed him, lifted them with optimistic lies, or figgerin' plans in the middle of disaster, or vinegar sarcasm in the valley of hopelessness. He was a gut fighter, plain and simple. He meant to gut it out. He knew the fighter traveled on the size of fight and spirit in him; not on mourning his plight, or dwelling on his doom. It was the way of Josey Wales.

He stood over them for a moment, looking down at this camp of weak and wounded. Striding to the saddle-bags on the horses, he fixed nose bags of grain for them, and returned with canteens and food.

Pitching a long round of jerky beef and two soured biscuits at Ten Spot's feet, he said, "Start chewing and swallerin'. It'll gripe yer belly, but ye keep at it. Ye've got to git strength. We'll need all ye got in ye."

Ten Spot began to chew. First he gagged and almost vomited, but the hard eye of Josey Wales was on him. He swallowed.

He tossed a canteen at the feet of Pablo, and with it a shirt he had taken from the bags. "Clean 'er up."

"*All* of 'er?" Pablo asked timidly.

"*All* of 'er, toenails to head," Josey said grimly.

With bashful trepidation, Pablo pulled away the covering blanket from the unconscious girl. Wetting the shirt from the canteen, he washed away the blood. As he worked, he spoke to her softly in Spanish, his tone that of the gentle corn raiser, sympathetic, soothing, apologetic, as he cleaned between and down her legs.

She regained consciousness, but as was the way of the Apache, she kept her eyes slit-closed, first to learn into what hands she had fallen, and if necessary to take advantage of the knowledge that her wits were alive, which her enemies would not know. Her hand still gripped the long knife.

She saw the white-eye, Ten Spot, who too had been a prisoner. He appeared free and was eating. She listened to the soft, soothing words of Pablo as he cleaned her body with the tenderness she had not known. She watched, listened, for a long time.

Suddenly she lifted the knife, flipped it expertly, circling in the air, and handed it, handle first, to the startled Pablo. He had not known, and still didn't, how close he had come to death.

He shook his head. "No," he whispered, and smiled. She was to keep the knife.

Standing, Josey Wales watched Aldamano. There was no activity that he could see through the long-glass. He took the chance. At any moment, the guards could be discovered, but he had to put his band in the best shape possible to ride.

He dug the "outlaw oven" in the ground, broke tiny dry sticks and set the fire. From a canteen, he poured water into a tin cup, cut chunks of jerky beef into it and set it to boil. He prepared another cup. When he had boiled the strength of the beef in both cups, he laced them with tequila, handing one to Ten Spot. The other he carried to the sleeping Chato.

Kneeling, he tenderly lifted the vaquero's head and shook him awake. While Chato weakly protested the scalding liquid, he poured it into him. "Swaller! er I'll pistol-whip yer haid!"

Precious minutes were ticking away, fifteen, thirty, but it would do no good to rush wildly away on horseback. His people would collapse in fifteen miles.

He motioned Pablo to take the cups and jerky beef and prepare broth for himself and the girl. But she was already dragging herself, elbow pulling, to the canteens, pouring water and cutting beef into them. She couldn't walk, or crawl. The huge swollen lump in her crotch made her legs splay like stiff crutches. She gave no indication of pain.

Josey watched her briefly. "Saint!" he said quietly.

"Her name," Pablo said, "she have told me, is En-lo-e. She know Escobedo will be coming. She say she will help, and when she cannot, she will roll into the brush, not to slow us." Pablo looked beseechingly up at Josey. "She will not slow us?"

"No," Josey answered softly, "she won't slow us. She'll do."

Josey had raised the quietly cursing Chato to a sitting position, lifting the bloodied bandages and inspecting the raw holes in his chest and back. Ten Spot sat, chewing, gagging, swallowing.

Josey squatted amongst them. "Watch!" he said, "and listen, 'special you, Chato, as was blowing around 'bout you knowed this here country sich as yer hand."

He placed a stick upright in the ground on the eastern side of the circle, another at the west. He drew a line from one to the other.

Pointing at the eastern stick, he said, "Thet there's Coyamo, sixty miles to our east. This here," he pointed to the western stick, "is Aldamano. We're right chere at this west end."

He rose for a moment, took a sweeping look through the long-glass at Aldamano. Without comment on what he had seen, he squatted again. "Them forty Rurales ain't got to Coyamo yit," he said, working his jaws slowly on a tobacco plug. " 'Nother hour fore they git there, riding hard; then they got a hour fight, maybe two—them bandidos is tough. Before they git the story about Pancho Morino, and me killing him." He paused, spat, listened to Pablo whispering in Spanish to En-lo-e what he was saying, "that's two, maybe three hour afore they find out what it's all about."

"Wait!" Chato chortled weakly, "wait until Valdez discover who was the messenger. Por Dios! I would like to see his face."

"Ye'll git to see it, if ye don't shet up," Josey snapped. With studied concentration, he began again. "Then there's

Valdez setting a good five hour from here. He'll ride like hell thisaway to tell Escobedo. Thet figgers—seven, maybe eight hour from Valdez' end—figgerin' thataway . . ."

"Sounds like we're not in bad shape," Ten Spot cut in, between gags of chewing.

"We're in bad shape," Josey said. "Fust trouble ain't coming from Valdez. At best figgerin' we got . . . ," he paused, looking at the sky, "three hour until somebody runs acrost them dead guards. Our fust trouble's coming from this end, right where we got our tails a-settin'." He spat on the hot coals. They hissed and filled the air with rancid tobacco smell.

"Let's say," he contemplated the sky, "thet it takes Escobedo thirty minutes to figger out the whole thing, him being a smart sonofabitch. Then he's a-goin' to send trackers circling the town to cut our trail. Thet's a hour. They'll find it. Thet's four hour, cutting out the thirty minutes. He'll saddle every man he's got and hit our trail. He'll send a man riding to meet Valdez and tell him to turn northwest, trying to cut us off, and meet him follerin' us—thet is . . . ," and he paused ominously, "if he ain't done caught us by then."

"We got to ride north?" Ten Spot asked.

"Well," Josey said, "we damn shore cain't ride east, er west, lessen ye want to go south and take a little sight-seeing of Mexico City, picking up a couple thousand Rurales alongst the way. North it's got to be."

Chato leaned forward, grunted at the pain, and with his finger drew a sloping line in the dust. "Straight north," he said, "the Rio Grande slopes from the north . . . south-east. Straight north . . . we will be forever in Mexico. Somewhere we must turn northeast, so we will hit the bend of the river, as she dips deep into Mexico. It will cut sixty . . . seventy miles off our run to the border."

Josey studied the line. "Fust time," he said quietly, "I

have ever heard a lick o' sense come out'n that cow-trailing head o' yourn. We head north, forty, fifty mile; we find a good place where it's rocky, rough; we switch northeast."

"Remember, Josey," Chato said weakly, "when time comes . . ."

"I remember, about yer goddamned borrerin' aheadst yer wages," Josey snarled.

Chato laughed, and grunted at the pain. "Once more, before we leave, Josey . . . a little of the . . . medicine would help."

Josey uncorked the bottle of tequila. Chato gulped the fiery liquor. As he brought the bottle down, Ten Spot reached and took it from him. "I need a slurp of that. My belly is tied in a knot." He turned up the bottle and drank.

"Remember," Chato said earnestly, his tongue thickening, "that is Pancho's bottle from which we drink; mine is for me, in the saddlebag."

"We'll all be shore and rec'lect thet," Josey said drily, "whilst we set here and drink it up. When Mr. Escobedo rides up, we'll remind him too thet Chato's bottle ain't to be tetched." He stood again with the long-glass and watched Aldamano.

"Time to move," he said tersely. He helped the staggering Chato aboard his big gray, lashing his feet in the stirrups. Ten Spot mounted the dapple unassisted. Color had come back into his face; he felt stronger.

While they had talked, Josey watched curiously while En-lo-e crawled to a mesquite bush. Using the knife, she cut it. Now she spoke to Pablo and he brought the rope from his saddle horn.

She tied one end of the rope to the brush. Pablo clumsily, but tenderly, sat her on his saddle, not astride, but sideways. He mounted behind her on the grulla, and holding her in the crook of his arm while he held the reins, he stood his horse, waiting for Josey to mount.

Josey took a last look at Aldamano. All seemed quiet. He swung aboard the roan and led the way, holding the reins of Chato's horse, the vaquero weaving in the saddle. Behind came Ten Spot, and bringing up the rear was Pablo with the Apache girl. Pablo had dressed her with his peon shirt. It hung on her small figure like a billowy poncho, to her knees.

Josey glanced backward. The girl had taken the reins of Pablo's horse. With his one arm, he held her. Josey noted that she did not drop the brush behind them, to cover the tracks. He knew what she would do. She would wait until they had ridden far to the north, where they would turn northeast, perhaps at a rocky gulch, a slate-side arroyo. Josey Wales would find that spot to turn.

For she knew Escobedo would find this camp. He would know they could not fly away from it, and so would follow the trail; but once they turned in the rocks, if they could reach them, to the northeast, she would drag the brush behind them.

It could take Escobedo's riders an hour, maybe two, riding north, circling to pick up the clear tracks, before they realized the brush had changed the trail.

Josey Wales felt a warmth for this Apache girl. Guerrilla natural-born. She figgered the edge.

And through the deepening darkness before dawn, they rode slowly, walking the horses. A pitiful pace that ticked away the sparing minutes before discovery. The minutes counted now, like drops of blood, for a limping, weakened, wounded band whose chances of reaching the Rio Grande were impossible.

Josey Wales could have made it alone easily; perhaps Pablo. The thought had not entered their minds. The bond of loyalty was stronger than life. Than death.

13

How many times the life of a man is determined by the smallest decisions!

When Josey Wales rescued Ten Spot and the Apache girl, En-lo-e, he had pushed Ten Spot over the wall of Aldamano first, and by so doing, saved his own life.

When he had come over the wall with En-lo-e, the Apache warriors, watching, had moved forward to kill him and take the girl. But Na-ko-la touched the arm of their leader. "That is Señor Sonofabitch he has rescued, and so is saving our sister as well." And so they sank back into the darkness of the bush and watched.

When the Rurales had rushed out of Coyamo, Na-ko-la had listened from his grave in the dungeon. All was quiet, and he raised his head. The door was open. It was a simple matter to uncover himself, slip through the door and into the desert.

Naked, he had run in the half circle, and finding the toe marks of his band, had caught them halfway to Aldamano. He told them of Sonofabitch, and how he had helped to save him, even when the Mexicanos had beaten him and kicked him; how he had laughed and would not tell that Na-ko-la lay hidden at their feet.

Friend or enemy, the Apache never forgot. The leader motioned two warriors to follow Josey Wales. In an hour they reported back: the tender care of En-lo-e by Pablo, the plans of the little band led by Josey Wales, the direction north they were taking. Their leader grunted. He said nothing.

They were a large band, for Apache. An Apache band, more often than not, was made up of five. Even two Apache warriors could spread terror through the countryside. This band numbered twenty-two.

They were not a raiding party, a food party. A raiding party sought horses, mules, cattle, and killed only when necessary. This was a blood party. These were the husbands, fathers, sons and brothers of the murdered women and children, butchered and scalped by Escobedo's Rurales. Their mission was not food. Blood for blood. The Code of the Apache.

The Code had been handed down—a hundred, two hundred years, so far in the dim past, they did not know—from father to son, mother to daughter.

The great Spanish nation had moved in on the Americas with their Conquistadores, masters of warfare, born, raised and bathed in two hundred years of war. They smashed the mighty Inca Empire in a matter of months. The Inca, with an economic and judicial system equal to Rome's, with commerce and balanced trade, with stone-paved highways where ten horses could ride abreast for a thousand miles.

The Conquistadores ground it all beneath their steel in months and made peons of the Inca, peons who died by the thousands, the hundreds of thousands.

The Spanish soldiers and priests had piled priceless records and artwork in mounds large as cities and burned them, making a mystery of the Inca's beginning, destroying the knowledge, the temples, the origins, everything.

With them, they brought the advanced stage of barbarism our historians call "civilization." They forced the peons to pay tribute to the god representing pain and death who hung from the cross; and the peon did, feeling sorry for this god, but secretly holding on to his past, the gods who did not promise with the threat of eternal fire and torture.

Northward the steel foot came, crushing the Mayan, the Zapotec, and finally—as climactic, irrefutable proof that the Conquistador was unconquerable—the majestic Aztec Empire.

Raping, pillaging for gold and silver, torturing revelations from the victims for more of the hidden metal; enslaving, setting up the system of politico-priest to create a gigantic bureaucracy of State and Church. And the Indian died.

He died in the mines of silver, enslaved in the fields, at the whipping posts, in the dungeons, at the stocks. The Indians starved on the meager rations, and were ravaged by the thousands as the diseases, attacking the weakened bodies like maggots, cut them down, as the scythe cuts the countless stalks of wheat.

The Indian learned. For survival, he learned to withdraw within himself, to touch his forehead in obedience to his masters, to bend his knee in humble submission, to become the silent, "dumb" peon. He was Christianized, conquered. His heritage and culture, his history and religion, his accomplishments and creativity forever destroyed, crushed beyond resurrection.

The masters of war and civilized barbarism moved north. No Aztec Empire stood in their path, no Inca, no organization. They had conquered even the jungle, here there was no jungle. But their plans became plans on paper. The steel foot stumbled; then it was halted. The masters of war met the Apache. Northward they could move no more.

The Apache invented a new kind of war, a war that made fumbling, frustrated novices of the great Conquistadores and their descendants. Guerrilla.

At first the Apache had met the Spanish, as had all the Indians of Mexico, with open hand. They came to the little towns that were rising in the north. They traded. The priests told them of their god, how they must pay tribute. The politicians gave them mescal, and while they were drunk, butchered them and their wives and children. The captured were tortured and enslaved. The Apache retreated.

No more did he plant his corn field. To come back to it for the harvest was to be ambushed by the Spanish soldier. He moved his mind further toward the mystic of his father, Usen of nature, and he moved his people back, back into the Mother Mountains, the Sierra Madre.

She stretched Her spine far into New Mexico and Arizona. Two thousand miles She plunged into Mexico, a hundred miles wide, thousands of miles of Her children. The Apache trails ran through secret passages where no horse could go. It was said that deep, high, within Her bosom, She nestled beautiful, fertile, hidden valleys of water and grass; but no Spaniard knew. To enter the

Sierra Madre of the west was death. None had ever crossed it. Only the Apache.

The white historian sought to designate the Apache tribes: the Chiricuahua, the Mescalero, the Tonto, the Membreno. But they became confused, for the Apache was the creator of the first rule of guerrilla warfare, later to be studied at the "civilized" war colleges without credit to the Apache. They broke up into small bands within the principal tribes: the Nedni Apache, the Bedonkohe, the Warm Springs—so many. The confusion lasts today.

Small bands came together for war and food objectives, then disseminated after the operation, and reassembled at small rancherias.

If attacked by a superior force, they fled in all directions, confusing the attacker, but always knowing the designated place to reassemble—a secondary, even a third, rendezvous point.

Never the frontal assault. Never the naive heroics of standing to the death; flee—run—hide. Think out the thoughts of the attacker; patience, wait, strike him when he is lulled in his mind, at the disadvantage. Hit his flanks, his rear—run.

The double-think: first your thoughts, then the thoughts of the enemy: what he is thinking, his habits, his way of life, his treacheries; then return to your own planning, based upon the thinking, the plans, of the enemy.

Move. Always move the rancherias. A moving target is hard to plan campaigns against, almost impossible to grasp.

Still they gathered the juniper berries high in the mountains, massaging them into sweetish rolls; gathered the acorns, shelled and made them into meal. But now the principal food must come from the raid. No more could the crops be raised. A field was stationary; it could not be moved. It was a trap of death.

Only the Apache exacted tribute from the Spanish,

who had forced millions of Indians to grind away their lives in payment of tribute to Spanish bureaucracy and the Church. Only the Apache.

And so the generations were raised from the day of each child's first step; the way of life was guerrilla.

The Apache warrior could run seventy miles a day, go five days without food. When he drank from a waterhole and slaked his thirst, he filled his mouth with water, and after four hours of running, he swallowed it. It carried him fifty more miles without the swelling of his tongue.

He never camped by a waterhole, always far away from it; enemies came to waterholes. He never sought the shade of a tree on the plains, or a bush large enough to shade a man. Pick the bush large enough only for the rabbit, talk to the bush, love the bush; become part of the bush, and it will become part of you. The Mexicanos and the white-eyes then will not see you. And they didn't.

When the soldados were sighted, patrolling the plains, send warriors ahead. Within the hour, a frightened Apache would leap and run three hundred yards ahead of the soldados; and they on horseback would run him down, zigzagging, into the open plain where there could be no ambush. But as they almost reached him with their lances, Apache rose from the living graves in the ground and pulled the soldados from their horses and killed them. Ambush where there can be no ambush.

And so the vast lands to the north would remain vacant: Texas, Arizona, New Mexico, Nevada. California could be settled only on the coast, where the ships could bypass the Apache. And the vast territory would fall like ripe fruit into the hands of the United States, the white-eyes who moved in.

The Apache would receive no credit in the United States books of history, for his stopping the Spanish movement northward. He would have no part in writing it.

He welcomed the white-eyes with friendship. He was invited to feasts, and the food was laced with strychnine, killing the Apache in agony. Old Mangus Coloradas, Chief of the Warm Springs Band, would seek peace and be captured under the white flag of truce, tortured with hot irons by United States soldiers and murdered with his hands tied behind his back. The officer-in-charge would receive a promotion.

Now the Apache fought on two fronts. The United States and Mexican governments had agreed: "eliminate" the Apache, man, woman, child, as advocated by the Sheridans, the Shermans. But now, one of those fronts was at the back of the Apache. The United States Army.

The U.S. Army, as treacherous as the ambitious officers who thirsted for victories and promotions; the politicians who fevered to embellish their records by advancing "civilization." As treacherous as the newspaper editors who screamed for more troops at the behest of men who hungered for the yellow gold. As treacherous as the men who sold the ammunition and supplies to the Army and must have the "war." The Apache had experienced it all before.

Though orators sounded in the "civilized" halls of their parliaments with speeches on the holy cause of "freedom"; though the scribes, with deep and moving phrases, wrote of this cause for mankind—it was the Apache, for generations, who had lived on the thin line of death, running, hiding, fighting, raiding, moving; who had fought for, and only for, this "freedom." Freedom from government! Freedom from the tributes, the taxes, the regulations, the parasite bureaucrats—the inevitable bureaucracy that sucked man dry of his spiritual self and ground him, rotting his soul with ambition for money, prestige, power; all the currents of storm and hell that man moves above the Mother Earth.

The Apache would receive no footnote on history's page

for this cause. He would be written as the "murderous renegade." The Apache would have no pen to touch the page of history.

Now the Apache band outside Aldamano moved closer to their leader. They asked him nothing. They simply waited for his decision. His wife and child had escaped the butchery; still he had been chosen to lead.

For nearly ten years, he had been the principal war leader. Ten years ago, he had returned to a butchery at his band's rancheria. There he had found his first wife, his slender, beautiful, frail Alope, raped so repeatedly that the female organ was unrecognizable, a huge lump pushing outward. Her tiny breasts had been cut from her and stuffed in her mouth. He had found his three children who, bellies sliced open by the Spanish soldados' sabers, had dragged themselves over the ground, snagging their entrails on the rocks. Dying as they had reached the body of their mother.

He had loved them deeply, as the Apache loves, without fault. He had burned all that had belonged to them. He had walked down to the river and he had stood, and the mysticism he had felt in his childhood grew in him.

He had walked into the desert and grown with the spirits—into the mountains—and it was said he was seen dancing with the mountain "gans," the spirits.

His flawless love had become the flawless diamond of hard hatred, pure as the love that gave it birth.

It was known he could talk to the wolf and the coyote. That the mesquite whined its secrets to him on the wind. More than once he had saved war parties from soldados.

One time, caught on the open plain, he and ten warriors were surrounded by two hundred soldados. He had turned to face the light breeze that sang in the bush. Softly he had sung his wind song. The breeze lifted to a wind; more he sang. The wind grew stronger; its temper became furious, whipping the desert into a storm, blinding the soldados. Every Apache had escaped. More than once he had done this. They knew. They had seen. His word was never questioned on the trail of blood.

Now he retreated from his warriors. He knew they wanted to strike Aldamano. It lay like a juniper nut before them, ready to be gathered. He went back into the brush and sat down alone.

He faced first to the east and softly sang, then to the south, the west, the north. He sat a long time. Slowly he rose and came back.

They would not hit Aldamano. He saw ahead, two, three days. He would lead them to that rendezvous. He yawned, and again, and again.

White men would misspell his Apache name. They would not be able to catch the soft, liquid talk of the Apache. Some would write he was called Go-klah-ye; others, Go-yak-la. The name meant "One Who Yawns." He had learned it long ago—the yawn that helped his mind to the alertness, to prepare it for the visions.

He motioned three warriors to him and gave them instructions. Quietly they slipped away. He squatted alone and waited, a short, powerfully built man, with black eyes that burned.

History would not know how to "classify" his Apache standing. He was not a chief. He held no official position. He was not a medicine shaman. But the white man's history makes no allowance for the mystic, the spiritual. They would write him off as a murderous renegade. They would wonder at his power and be confused. But they would not misspell the name given him by the Mexicanos. He was Geronimo.

Quietly the Apaches crouched. They were out of rations and waited for the three warriors. They came, leading the mule.

As ghosts, they had slid among the Rurales. With raw-hide strips, they tied the mule's legs together, leaving him only a short stride. With another strip, they pulled down his head.

A shuffling head-down mule is obviously grazing. As he moves clumsily along, stopping here and there, he attracts no attention. Patiently he was moved into the shadows, and away from the Rurales as easily as a riverboat gambler slides a card from the bottom of a deck.

They led the mule a mile to the northward, where they butchered him, each cutting the pieces he desired into strips for his food sack. They ate. Then rising without a word, they followed their leader, Geronimo, in the rhythmic, shuffling stride toward the northeast, the same direction as the little band of Josey Wales.

Their soft shuffling moccasins, the light grunting of their throats, brought a rise in the wind. Some range riders would have recognized the sound. It was sometimes heard, and called viento de muerte, the "death wind."

14

The pace was slow. In the darkness, Josey turned his head to watch the stride of the gray, carrying Chato. The stride was long, smooth. He stepped up, by the slightest gait, the smooth, long walk of his roan. Just under the trot. A jolting trot would jar the jagged wound that ran through the body of Chato. He would bleed inside. And he would die.

Josey judged the walk, four, maybe five miles an hour. He watched the sky and counted away the time. One hour, two, three hours, and the wind rose in the blackness, morning wind that breathed harder before birthing the day. Soon it would be sunrise.

The light shot upward on their right, wiping away the

stars, and the sun burst, exploding over the rim of the plain. Ahead of him Josey could see waves of flat, endless mesquite. The plain.

He turned, not halting, and tried to look backward toward Aldamano, but could not see it on the flat surface. At best, an hour before Escobedo's Rurales, circling the town, would cut their trail. Escobedo would send the messenger to meet Valdez, instructing Valdez to turn northwest and meet him on the trail north.

He cut a tobacco plug and chewed slowly. Figgerin' high, it would give 'em twenty-five miles before Escobedo would take the trail after them. He'd be crazy mad, messing up his plans. He'd ride his Rurales like hell was on their tail. Josey Wales chewed and figgered. It was a tight corner they was in. He spat, topping a lizard's head resting in the shade of cactus.

Once he turned and snarled at Chato, "By God, it's a pleasing thing, jest to ride along without'n yore big mouth running off."

Chato, his head sagging, sombrero dragging the neck of the horse, raised his head. It was an effort. His head waggled, but white teeth flashed in a weak smile. "Si," he whispered, "don't worry for me, Josey. I can ride." The sombrero dropped; head down again.

"I ain't worrying none about ye," Josey said. "Yore damn belly-shot condition is improving of yer ways, is all I was remarking."

The sun rose, hotter. Ten Spot weaved only slightly in the saddle. His colorless eyes stayed steadily on the back of Chato.

Three hours, Josey figgered. Three hours and Escobedo would be on their backs. His eyes scanned the plain ahead—flat, not even a damn place to hole up. Without slackening the pace, he pulled the long-glass from his bag, looking ahead now for anything, a butte, even a good-sized rock, by God. There was nothing. The mesquite waving in the wind, the cactus, the ocotillo and gamma grass.

The sun had tilted past noon. Every fifteen minutes, Josey raised the glass and scanned the prairie ahead. For an hour. And then he picked it up—a thin wavering line off to their right, a shallow arroyo running from the north that petered out on the plain. He slanted the horses toward the arroyo.

Now with the glass he looked back. First he saw nothing, then the cloud of dust, a big cloud growing larger, moving fast.

"Escobedo," he muttered beneath his breath. The sun slanted another hour toward the west when they reached the arroyo. He stopped the horses. It was a disappointment.

Narrow, its sides gravel and small rocks, so shallow it would barely hide a man's head on horseback, standing on the sandy bottom. It wavered and twisted northward, a runoff for the water of rare cloudbursts. Josey led them down into the ditch, for it was only a ditch, sliced in the prairie. With their horses standing on the bottom, they could not see the prairie.

"We can hold them here, Josey," Chato said.

"Hold 'em, hell," Josey said. "They'll lay back and potshot, circle us and wait on Valdez. With sixty Rurales, they'll splatter us all over these here rocks."

Pablo and the girl started to dismount.

"Everybody stay on yer hoss," Josey said. "Git out the jerky and be eating while I'm telling ye . . ."

"And Pancho's bottle," Chato interrupted, "it is still half filled. My bottle . . ."

"I know," Josey snapped, "your'n ye're saving."

Ten Spot took the bottle, Pancho's, from his saddlebag. It was half full. He raised it and swallowed long, passing it to Chato. The vaquero swallowed great gulps, lowered the bottle and smacked his lips, "Bueno." Pablo shook his head. He had tried the tequila before and found nothing bueno in it. They ate on the jerky.

" 'Pears," Josey chewed slowly, "this here is the way it is. The hosses need water bad, and graining."

Chato, briefly revived by the tequila, pointed to the northeast.

"Twenty, maybe thirty mile, there is a hacienda grande. We . . ."

"All right," Josey said, "here's what ye do. Pablo, give me yore sombrero." Pablo took off the hat and passed it to Josey. "I want all the blankets; and I'll need yore coat, Ten Spot." The gambler asked no question. He shucked the coat, leaving him half naked in the sun.

"Now," Josey said, dismounting and rolling the blankets behind his saddle, "ye all wait right here. When ye hear Escobedo and his men riding by, ye wait fifteen, twenty minutes; then ye head northeast. Pablo, ye tell the girl everything I'm saying. Let her lead; 'Pache knows how. Ten Spot, ye mind after Chato; lead his hoss; no trot, er Chato will die."

"There will be no trot, Josey," Ten Spot said flatly, "even if they're on our tail."

"Now . . . ," Josey cut tobacco and chewed, "tie the rope to Chato's hoss. Let it drag the bresh behint ye, might be it'll help; but drag slow, no dust. When ye git to the hayseenda," he cocked his eye at the sun, "it'll be after dark. Ye wait in the bresh, maybe three hour. If I ain't there in four hour, I won't be coming more'n likely. Go in, take yer chances."

He walked to the side of the arroyo and with the long knife slashed three heavy mesquite branches. Walking to the roan, he lifted the rope from his saddle horn. One end of the rope he tied to the pile of mesquite he had cut; the other he wrapped securely around his saddle horn. When he had finished, he walked beside Chato, lifting his shirt, inspecting the bandages and wounds. They were bleeding.

"What you do, Josey?" Chato asked.

Josey spat on a rock. "Me and Big Red is aiming to take a little ride." He checked the sun. "We're going to ride hour, two hour, straight north. Me and Big Red is going to ride so hard the dust cloud will look like we're all skeered out'n our head, and breaking fer a last run. Mr. Escobedo, he's going to figger he's jest about got us proper. After that," Josey sighed, "well, it'll git dark. They cain't track in the dark. Me and Big Red will meet ye sometime tonight at the hayceenda."

He didn't mention what they all knew. Pulling the heavy mesquite, could the roan last an hour? Two hours? If he stepped in a hole, broke a leg, stumbled, it would be over for Josey Wales.

It was a death ride. Every one of them knew it. Even the girl; for softly in Spanish, Pablo had told her.

They were receiving new life, a night of non-pursuit. A chance for this little band of weak and wounded, where there had been no chance.

Josey shook the hand of Chato. The tequila and the emotional nature of the vaquero made tears run unashamedly down his face. "This," he whispered brokenly, "this . . . Josey . . . should not be, we should not part, we . . ."

"Shet up, ye cow-trailing drunk. I'm glad to git shet of ye."

Ten Spot said nothing. He gripped Josey's hand hard. Pablo held his hand long and prayed silently. En-lo-e leaned from the saddle to touch him as he passed.

He leaped on the roan and rode out of the arroyo. At the top, he pulled the long-glass, and now could plainly see the Rurales. He figgered them to be thirty, maybe twenty minutes away.

He slid the glass back into the saddlebag, cut a chew of tobacco into his cheek.

"Vaya con Dios!" The voice of Pablo floated up from the arroyo.

"Same to ye," said Josey Wales. He pulled his hat low. "All right, Big Red," he growled, "Let's see if'n ye still got it in ye!"

The big roan jumped, jerking at the huge roll of mesquite. He strained, leaping into a run, and his ears came backward until they lay flat. Big Red, like Josey Wales, did not cotton to sich as figgered he couldn't do.

Ten Spot had crawled to the top of the arroyo. "By God!" he exclaimed, "that dust cloud looks like an army running for the border." He looked back and could see the Rurales coming, shouting now, triumphant; they had jumped the rabbits in the open brush!

As he rode, Josey guided the roan with his knees, trying to keep him in the open. He shortened the rope, pulling the mesquite almost to the heels of the horse; it gave him better control to keep from snagging on the brush.

Now, at intervals, he lifted the mesquite entirely off the ground, creating puffs of dust instead of the steady roll. Each time he lifted, it gave a few seconds respite from the pulling to the roan—a very small edge.

The Rurales' horses drummed closer to the arroyo, and they thundered past where the little band couched over their horses. Some of them had drawn their rifles and were shooting at Josey. Then, as thunder rolling over the prairie, disappearing in a fading rumble, the sound of their horses was gone.

Pablo and the girl led; Ten Spot, leading Chato, followed; out of the arroyo, northeast away from the pursuit, walking slowly, quietly in the wind. Their thoughts were on the desperate chase to the north. Each knew that ride was giving them their lives.

Pablo prayed for the scar-faced bandido, Josey Wales. Even if it was, as said by the priests, that the bandido had no soul, he asked the Santos and God to guide the feet of the roan so he would not stumble, he would not fall.

Eyes narrowed against the sunlight, Josey Wales picked the ground ahead for the big horse, pressing first with the left knee, then the right. The roan responded cat-quick.

For thirty minutes it was a horse race, the roan slowly losing. The Rurales, excited over jumping their quarry, were charging at dead heat. Slowly they gained ground. But they could not hold it. Big Red had been walking all day. The horses of the Rurales and Escobedo had already been driven hard. There was, too, the matter of the roan's big heart and will. The Rurales began to fade.

At the end of an hour they were far behind, forced to slow the horses or kill them. Josey pulled down the roan into a low gallop. He did not want to move too far ahead, neither did he want to exhaust the big horse under him. Already froth blew back from the bits and sweat was ringing the saddle blanket. He dropped the pace slower. Always he kept the arroyo to his right, as it wound snake-like to the north.

The sun fell, losing heat, turning the prairie a bloody red through the dust haze, and then dropping behind the jagged rim of the Sierra Madre. Twilight came. With it came the evening wind. Josey brought the roan to a stop.

Far behind, still they came, dragging at a slow pace; but Escobedo, he knew, would bring them on. He hooked a leg loosely around the horn of the saddle. He was covered with dust. Plug-cutting his tobacco, he commenced his slow chewing. "Let's see, Red," he told the heaving horse, "they'll figger us to be run out, 'cause they are too. They got to figger we'll try to stop and hide in the dark—only chanct we got, hosses dead under us, and sich. Time they git to where we're setting at, it'll be total dark."

Settling his foot in the stirrup, he dropped the horse down into the shallow arroyo and up the other side. Ten yards back, he tied him to a mesquite, filled a nose bag with grain and set it over the horse's mouth. "Might's well be stuffing up, last we got," he reminded the horse.

He moved quickly, pulling the blankets, the sombrero, Ten Spot's coat that he had rolled behind the saddle. He walked down into the arroyo. He draped the coat around a mesquite bush and set the sombrero atop. Stepping back, he admired his handiwork. "Right as rain," he opined softly.

Taking the blankets, he cut, and rolled in each of them, a small mesquite: lumpy, blanketed figures that slept on the ground. He cut a long stick and leaning it in the mesquite that held the sombrero and coat, he stepped back admiringly. "Damned if'n ye don't look jest like ye was guarding, though 'pears like ye've hunkered down and gone to sleep, ye sorry bastard."

He knelt and built a small fire and dropped jerky beef into it, filling the air with the smell of burnt meant. He stomped the fire out. "The smell'll bring 'em, fire looks liken to be a trap . . ." He talked conversationally with himself as he worked.

The twilight deepened. The brightest star came out. He ran to his horse. Reeling in the mesquite brush, he untied it and rolled his rope around the saddle horn. Mounting the roan, he recrossed the arroyo and rode back in the direction of Escobedo's troops, turned after a hundred yards and came back, down into the camp he had made; round and round, he rode the horse, stomping the ground, then up the opposite side, and disappeared into the bush.

For the common outlaw, this would have been enough. Chances were that the Rurales, unable to track in the night, would simply encamp until morning, waiting to pick up the trail. But Josey Wales was no common outlaw, he was a warrior-guerrilla. There was the slightest chance they might circle, carefully looking; might have an Indian to determine the tracks of the roan going east. Josey Wales meant to take the edge off the chance.

He walked, leading the horse a hundred yards south, toward the direction the Rurales would come, but opposite them on the bank of the arroyo.

Tying the roan back in the bush, he lifted two '44's from the holsters on his saddle and came back to the arroyo. He picked a spot at the very edge beneath a small bush and lay forward, propped on elbows, the .44's already cocked.

Ye could figger the military bastards. When they spotted the camp, they would send out flankers to encircle it. They would cross the arroyo a hundred yards to the north of the camp, and figgerin' from here, a hundred yards to the south. If Josey had lain directly opposite the camp, he would have been caught in the circle, first-grade stuff for Josey Wales.

Now he listened. The moon sliver had broadened, dropping a ghost light on the prairie, making a dim white strip of the sand on the bottom of the arroyo. Wind brought the faraway howl of the wolf and the yelp of the coyote.

He heard them. Tired horses, dragging their feet in the dust, the creak of leather. They were riding the very rim of the arroyo. They figgered, that being the only place to hide, there was a chance of their quarry trying to double back. On they came, the heaviness of the horse hoofs increasing.

Almost opposite him, across the arroyo, Josey heard a soft exclamation in Spanish. He grinned evilly. It was no coincidence that he lay at the very edge of the burnt-beef smell. All sound stopped.

Straining his ears, he listened for the whispered conference, men dismounting to sneak forward along the arroyo.

Ten minutes passed, a horse stomped, fifteen minutes. The scouts came back.

Softly they were whispering. He heard a large number of them scurrying alongside the bank of the arroyo, that would be the ones to go beyond the camp and cross the arroyo above it, and the ones to charge it from that side.

These across from him would give them time before they moved. Another fifteen minutes, twenty, and Josey strained his eyes. A figure came down the opposite bank, bent low, walking cautiously, followed by another and another.

They were coming almost directly to him. Still he waited, noting another and another. The first one was already scrambling up the bank in front of him. Couldn't wait too long, the sonofabitch would be stepping on his haid. Six in a line, he counted.

The first figure rose before him not five feet away. BOOM! The deep throat of the .44 echoed and knocked the Rurale backward. Before he hit the ground, the Colt hammer fell in Josey's right hand and had killed the second. The left-hand Colt boomed again; the third fell like a sack in the sand at the bottom. The figures behind them turned to run back up the bank; methodically, Josey thumbed the hammers, one, two, between the shoulder blades, and they pitched sprawling on the rocks. The last of them made it into the brush on the other side.

"Goddamn!" Josey spat in disgust.

He came to his knees, shoving the emptied Colts into his belt, and drew the two from his holsters. He fired, rapid fire, spacing his shots, walking them along the rim of the arroyo, until the guns were emptied. Bending, he ran, and taking the reins of the roan, walked slowly away to the east.

Behind him, bedlam was breaking loose. Rifles and pistols cracked and boomed, echoing in the arroyo, spitting fire first one way and the other. After walking a hundred yards, Josey mounted the roan and headed him east.

The shooting was dying down; now only an occasional shot. He heard shouted orders in Spanish coming faintly on the wind. Then all was quiet.

He kept the roan pointed east. After thirty minutes of easy trotting, he turned in the saddle; huge fires lit the night sky behind him. "Now thet," he reckined to the roan, "would be the signal set fer Mr. Valdez to make haste his tail-to."

In the silver moonlight, he slowly reloaded the pistols, and allowed himself a satisfied chuckle. "Why hell, Red," he drawled, "that there Escobedo wouldn't had lasted past breakfast in Missouri."

Josey figgered the way. He had ridden north. Chato had said they would ride northeast. He trotted the roan, figgerin' to double their slow gait, directly east. Though still deep in the enemy's territory, sure to be trailed come dawn, Josey Wales was feeling better about the whole damn thing. He permitted himself some light entertainment.

> "*I got a gal on Flywood Mountain*
> *Puritest gal in Tennessee*
> *Reckin come Sunday, I'll go a-courtin'*
> *Up thet mountain, m'hound and me.*"

The roan gave a disgusted snort. There was one thing Josey Wales could not do. He couldn't carry a tune in a bucket.

The Apache, leaving Aldamano, had run northeast too, but the tangent of their run carried them further north. Seldom did an Apache cross the plains in the light of day, and so at daybreak they had rested, crouched beneath the small bushes near the arroyo into which Josey Wales would ride.

They had watched the dust clouds coming with growing interest, moving farther back into the brush. Then they recognized the scar-faced white-eye who had rescued their sister.

In the purple of desert twilight, they had moved close, curiously watching him set up the false camp. They had moved back, behind him, to watch. They were bolder now. Usen had brought the night and dimmed the vision of the enemy.

They had watched it all. The staccato gunfire of Josey Wales, the confusion and firing of the Rurales as they moved in on the false camp. Then they faded away into the bush.

Admiration for the scar-face rose in the breast of Geronimo. How many times had the Apache tethered the useless pony, set the false camp, scattered the cooking utensils.

When the soldados had surrounded the camp for the ambush, the Apache had moved in to ambush the ambushers. The scar-face thought as the Apache.

Geronimo had no way of knowing: Josey Wales' raids in guerrilla warfare matched the number of his own.

Now the Apache did not follow Josey Wales. They set out toward the east, but running slightly toward the north. Geronimo had the vision of events to come. An edge of which Josey Wales knew nothing.

15

Two hours he lazily trotted Big Red. Chato had said there was fresh water at the hacienda. The roan wanted water, bad. Josey loosened the reins and let the roan have his head. The horse kept the same direction for a while, then his nose came up, his ears. He smelled the water, and altered their course, turning slightly to the north. Another hour. The roan picked up speed, falling into a rolling lope.

Josey scanned the landscape ahead. The white 'dobe of a big hacienda would show right smart in the moonlight. He didn't see it, and so with the increasing gait of the roan, he sent a piercing whistle, "SKEEEeeeeee!" the scream of the Tennessee nighthawk.

He stopped the roan and listened. There was only the wind. For another thirty minutes he let the roan have his head; and halted, whistling the same piercing sound, again, and again.

Faintly, from far away, he heard the whipping call of the whippoorwill, directly ahead.

The little band was not far; the whipping whistle had come from Chato, the weakness giving it the sound of distance.

They were camped in heavy bushes of mesquite as he rode among them. It was not much of a camp. There was no food, no blankets, no fire for warmth. Chato lay spraddled on the ground and around him sat Pablo, En-lo-e and Ten Spot.

Their horses were tied tightly together, held from the water smell by the tight grip of Pablo and En-lo-e. They stomped and snorted. Ten Spot was blistered; his face, shoulders, chest and back showed red, even in the moonlight.

As Josey swung from the roan, Ten Spot said sourly, "By God, I'll die 'fore I give away my coat again in the middle of the goddamn desert. And," he thumbed angrily at the sprawling Chato, "this crazy bastard thinks it's funny if he gets the chance to slap me on the back."

Pablo and the girl said nothing. It required nothing to be said. They were done. Another mile and they would drop in the desert, food for the buzzards.

Except Chato. He had placed his sombrero under his head, in lieu of a blanket, and his teeth flashed white. "It was an accident, I swear Josey . . . both times. Señor Ten Spot, how he jump!" The vaquero laughed weakly and coughed.

Josey cut a tobacco plug. With methodical, nerve-screaming slowness, he chewed. Ten Spot stood impatiently, feeling his chest and stomach. Josey spat and nodded toward the gigantic white lump rising two hundred yards to the north, "That there hayceenda—seen anybody abouts, coming er going?" he asked.

"No, Josey," Pablo said, "I have watch. Nobody. No guardia on the walls. But there is a light at the back, a candle. Part of the roof behind has been burned and fallen in . . . ," he shrugged, "the War."

Josey watched the hacienda for a long time. It was two-storied white adobe with a high wall fronting it that held a patio. He squatted on his boot heels and looked at Pablo. "Ye still got them peon sandals and britches in yer saddlebag?"

"Si," Pablo said.

"Tell ye what ye do," Josey said, "pull off them vaquero britches and boots and put them sandals and peon britches on. Let the girl keep the shirt, ye'll look more ragged without a shirt."

"I will?" Pablo asked. But he rose, went into the bushes and changed the clothes.

"How you figuring, Josey?" Ten Spot was becoming interested. Josey made no answer. He was watching the hacienda. Pablo came from the bushes, sandals on his feet, the white ragged pants he had worn as the beggar in Santo Rio. With no shirt, the stump of his arm hung pathetically. He was a sorry-looking figure.

"Good!" exulted Josey, "ye look jest right. Now tell ye what ye do. Ye go around to the back of that hayceenda. Ye knock politely on the door, like'n ye're scared . . ."

"I am scared, Josey," Pablo said humbly.

"Good," Josey continued, "ye jest keep knocking, polite, but keep at it—that way, ye more than likely won't git shot, as if'n ye was banging away at it." He paused, sorting out the thinking. "Then," he drawled, "when somebody opens the door, er winder, ye move into the light so's they kin see what a sorry-looking thing ye look like—which ye do. This will," Josey added emphatically, "more'n likely keep ye from gittin' shot agin."

Pablo shuffled his feet nervously and nodded.

"Ye tell 'em ye was with a mule train coming out of Coyamo, thet 'Paches jumped ye, ye're the onliest one got away. Tell 'em ye want to warn the bigshot there."

"The Don," Chato interrupted.

"All right, Mr. Don," Josey said, "so's he kin wake up his men and sich, as they 'pear to be coming thisaway." Josey was silent for a while. "This here will bring out whatever is hiding around in them rooms and bunch 'em up fer me. I'll be clost by."

Pablo crossed himself and a shudder ran over his body.

"Ye got it in yore mind now, how to knock, stand in the light, the story?" Josey looked hard at Pablo.

"Si," Pablo said softly, "but . . ."

"And tell 'em ye're hongry and sich. That'll sound natural," Josey added.

"I am hungry," Pablo said simply.

"Good," Josey said, "then ye're might near everything ye're making out to be. Won't be no trouble atall."

"But . . ." Pablo said.

"Git," Josey snapped softly, "vamoose!"

The Apache girl rose and fell, trying to follow Pablo. He turned; holding her hand, he explained in rapid Spanish. Still she tried to crawl after him.

Josey grabbed her arm brutally. "SET!" he snarled. She sat.

As Pablo walked hesitantly away, Chato called softly, "You are now, official, in the Josey Wales Messenger Service. Vaya con Dios!"

The half-joking words of Chato brought added weight to the heavy doom Pablo felt in his mind. So this was the way he was to die! He faltered, but then, stubbornly, he continued his slow walk, circling the hacienda to reach the door at the rear.

Josey knelt and watched intently the retreating back of Pablo. He was counting the steps to the hacienda.

"Josey?" came from Chato.

"Yeah?"

"How did you do . . . how did you manage to escape Escobedo?"

"I couldn't git but five of 'em," Josey spat. "Might near got another un, but . . ."

"*You* couldn't kill *but five!*" Ten Spot exclaimed. He jumped back to his feet. "How in hell did you kill . . ."

"Shet up," Josey drawled, "I'm a-countin' the ground to cover fer that hayceenda."

En-lo-e watched Pablo intently until he disappeared around the white wall.

Josey sat down. "Escobedo cain't foller the tracks now. He's set big fires, guiding Valdez to 'em. Come daylight, that's . . . ," he looked at the stars, "six hour, they'll be coming, sixty, er fifty-five, I put now, Rurales. Escobedo, he'll be madder'n a coon dog which treed a possum."

"Can we stand them off here, Josey?" Chato asked softly. "So many . . ."

"Ain't aiming to," Josey said. He rose in a half crouch. "I'll be sending Pablo back fer all of ye, er if I don't, shoot whatever comes thisaway."

With this terse advice, he left, running crouched, falling, rising to run again. Chato raised on his elbows; Ten Spot stood to watch. They could see, only dimly, the head rising, then falling, appearing as a bush that waves down, then rights itself in the wind. He disappeared into the shadow of the high wall.

Josey lay there. He heard no sound, the prairie wind, the tenor call of a coyote. Flat on the ground, he pulled himself slowly to the big open gate and cautiously looked inside.

A second-story veranda, with steps leading up from the patio, ran round the building. The patio was stone, unkept, weeds growing between the stone. Thick doors indicated rooms on the ground floor and second story.

He stood against the wall, and silently, quickly, he slid into the shadow of the veranda. Inching his way along the wall, he came to the back. The door was open and inside he heard voices—Spanish; he couldn't understand.

He edged away from the wall, backing further from the door where candlelight spilled out on the stone. Now a voice was raised in furious anger, and Josey heard the hard pounding of flesh on flesh. He moved again, and brought into view a small white-haired man, old, dressed in a silken night robe. He was standing, impassively watching something before him.

Josey stepped easily to his right. A big man, bull-shouldered, with long black hair, had his back to Josey. He was vaquero-dressed with high-heeled boots, and a white-handled pistol hung on his belt. It was he who was shouting. He held Pablo by the throat with one hand, and as Josey watched, brought a brutal fist down on Pablo's face, knocking him to his knees.

Pablo was trying to answer some question. His face was swelling from the blows. One eye was almost closed.

Then the vaquero felt the slight pressure on his spine; the click of the cocking .44 was unmistakable. He froze, fist in the air.

Josey Wales did not even look at him. With the cocked .44 in the vaquero's back, his eyes scanned the room. The old man stood as in shock. His eyes widened. Against the wall, two fat Indian women, servants, covered their faces.

As if inquiring of the weather, Josey casually addressed Pablo, struggling to his feet, "What they say, Pablo?"

Pablo spoke through swelling lips; blood ran from his mouth. "They say, Josey, their ladies are in Ciudad de Mexico, for safety. They say their riders are on the range, gathering up the cattle scattered by the—the Indian son-of-a-dog, Juarez. They are all who are here." Pablo wiped the blood from his mouth with his hand. One eye now was completely closed.

Josey eased the gun barrel away from the vaquero's back; as he did, the big man dropped his arm and turned to face Josey.

Josey's hand moved so fast he had no time to raise his arm in protection. The gun barrel of the heavy Colt flashed in a downward stroke. The vaquero fell like a log. The split in his hair showed white skull, and blood ran over the floor.

"That'll learn ye," Josey drawled, "what a Missouri slapping is liken to." The two servant women screamed and sat down, trembling against the wall.

Josey turned to the old man, who had not moved a muscle. "Ye speak English?" he asked conversationally.

The old man drew himself up proudly. "Much better than you, bandido! And French, and Spanish, and Ger . . ."

"All right," Josey drawled, "ye're eddicated. Set down in that there chair." The old man stood. With a boot, Josey kicked him sprawling into the chair. "SET!"

"Ye done right good there, Pablo," Josey praised, holstering the Colts. "Tell ye what ye do. Tell them two women to stoke up a fire in that big fancy stove they got there; fill them three wood tubs full of hot water. Tell 'em to put on plenty of vittles, and sich fer eating. Tell 'em pronto, er I'll shoot 'em in the haid."

Pablo spoke to the women softly; at the end of his talk, when he reached "the haid" part, they leaped to their feet and began to open the stove, setting a fire. Repeatedly they crossed themselves for the bandido who had no soul.

"Pablo," Josey spoke softly, "reckin ye can bring the others in. Be careful with Chato; too much jolting will bust him inside."

"Si." Pablo padded through the door and across the patio.

They were there in a matter of minutes. Chato unconscious from the pain of movement. Josey had him stretched on the table, and En-lo-e unwrapped the dirty bandages. The ugly wounds were not closing, but still, there was no fester, no infection.

At the appearance of En-lo-e, the servant women shrank back. "Apache!" they breathed; but Pablo instructed them, and they filled the tubs with hot water, brought clean bandages and salves for the wounds.

Pablo and Ten Spot stabled the horses in the barn at the rear, watering, graining them, and rubbing them down. They reported only two other horses in the barn.

Pablo spoke to En-lo-e. She stripped the long shirt from her body, and naked, stepped into the hot tub of water. She sat, luxuriating in its warmth, and slowly her head tilted backward, resting on the edge of the tub. She slept. The warmth of the water washed away the weariness, the aches, the pain, and the blood.

Josey sat down in a chair, facing the Don, while the women bathed Chato and dressed his wounds.

Ten Spot, washing, shaving away the beard, stepped back from the mirror. "By God! I feel more like a human again!"

"Since ye're feeling human," Josey said, "ye might sashay yore tail through Mr. Don's rooms and round up all the guns and ammunition."

"A good thought, for a human," Ten Spot smiled, bowing to the Don as he passed. He could be heard in the rooms, banging doors, pulling open closets.

The Don could stand it no longer. He stood erect. "This

—you disgrace my hacienda—plundering my belongings—
it—it . . ." He could find no words to express the indignity.
He sat down and held his head in his hands.

Pablo was slicing beef and rolling it into big chunks of
bread. He handed a roll to Josey. As he chewed, Josey
watched the Don narrowly.

"Mr. Don," he drawled.

The Don's head snapped up. "The *name*, bandido, is Don
Francisco de Garcia. Don is a title, not a name!"

"No need to git tetchy about it," Josey said soothingly.
"Like I was a-goin' to say," he took a large bite from his
beefed bread and chewed for a moment, "what ye got so
hell fixed agin' this here feller Juarez?"

Fire shot from the eyes of the Don. "Juarez," he said,
"is a pagan. A Zapotec Indian—El Presidente, indeed! He
will take all the land from the churches, the mines; he
says he will bring about land reform, as he calls it, which
means stealing part of my land and giving it to the Indians.
My land!"

Josey accepted another huge sandwich from Pablo and
began chewing again. "How much land ye got?"

"My land," the Don replied proudly, "would require
five days for a fast horseman to ride across."

Josey sat up in genuine amazement. "Lord Almighty, ye
don't say—and ye say, it's all yourn?"

"It is all mine," the Don announced.

After a long silence, Josey said, "Reckin with that much
land ye ain't never seed all of it."

"No, I haven't," the Don said, "but it is there."

"How'd ye manage to git all sich land?" Josey asked
curiously.

"The land, bandido," the Don answered, "was handed
down to me from my father, and his father before him, and
his before him."

"Where'd he git it? I mean the fust un?" Josey asked.

The Don looked puzzled. "Why, he conquered it, of course," he said.

"Never heerd tell of conquering land," Josey said around a mouthful of beef. "Plowing land, grazing it, sich . . ."

"The Indians," the Don said impatiently, brushing a thin hand through his white hair, "he conquered it from the Indians."

"Oh," said Josey Wales. "I see: he reformed it from the Indians, and this here Juarez feller is aiming to reform some of it back. Sounds reasonable."

The Don stared at this ignorant, murderous fool. "You are stupid apparently of all civilized procedure. It is useless to discuss it further." He dropped his head again into his hands.

"Well, reckin I am some ignorant, not gittin' schooling to speak of, but don't feel so bad about it, Mr. Don," he said comfortingly. "You'll have enough land which ye can ride around and see, git to like it, git taken to it. You and the Indians liable to git on jest fine, it ain't all that bad. My motto," he said, propping a boot heel on the belly of the brute lying before him and crossing his other boot comfortably over it, "is live and let live."

The Don, looking down at the figure on the floor, said sarcastically, "Yes, I can see it is your motto."

Ten Spot stepped into the room, a different man. He wore shined boots, a ruffled shirt with laced cuffs, and the black coat had velvet on the collar. "Almost," he said, "a perfect fit. When I am in, ah, better circumstances, Don Francisco, be assured I shall reimburse you for this generosity."

Josey looked coolly at the gambler. "Ye look exactly like a Kansas City pimp. How 'bout the guns?"

Ten Spot reached outside the door and brought forth a carbine. "It is the latest model," he said. "Cartridges . . ." He handed over a long belt of cartridges.

Josey felt the gun, smoothing his hands down the stock. A fine rifle.

"This here," he said, "put in the boot of Chato's saddle, and hang the cartridge belt on it. He's the best rifle shot."

Chato had awakened. Lying on the table, he raised himself on elbows. "You have never admitted so before this, Josey . . . always you have said, I was not . . . Remember?"

"I know," Josey snarled. "I jest said thet to keep Pablo from shooting hisself with it."

To Ten Spot, he said, "See if ye can cram something down that big mouth of his'n besides tequila. Like beef and bread, fer instance. I got a sneaking notion the reason he cain't stand up is his legs is full o' liquor."

It was Pablo that Josey assigned the first watch on the outside wall. The stoic Indian, strapping on the pistol belt, looked long at En-lo-e, still asleep in the tub.

"She's healing, son, and resting well," Josey said, almost tenderly. Pablo nodded. "Ten Spot will relieve ye in two hour," Josey said. "Take, and watch with care."

"I will watch," said Pablo, and faded into the darkness.

The candle burned lower. Ten Spot lay on the floor, Chato on the table. The two Indian servant women slept, crouched against the wall of the kitchen.

Slowly the old man raised his head a mere trifle. He looked cannily at the bandido seated across from him. There was a derringer upstairs, if he could reach it. For a long time he studied Josey Wales, chair propped against the wall, feet crossed on the belly of the foreman sprawled on the floor. The gray hat shaded the bandido's eyes. Were they open or closed? Beneath the shaded brim the deep scar jagged through the stubble of black beard. He seemed to be breathing easily, regularly.

With painful slowness, the old man raised himself from the chair. Once standing, he stood for a long time, gaining reassurance the bandido slept. Softly he took the first step toward the door. He merely blinked his eye, and the big hole was staring at his face; the .44 had moved magically, hammer clicking in the cock. He stood petrified. How had it moved so quickly!

The bandido said nothing, but the hole of the barrel followed the Don back to his seat, and as magically disappeared when he sat down. He was resigned.

Quietly he addressed the bandido. "Do you never sleep?" He sniffed. "Or bathe?"

The drawl came lazily from beneath the hat brim. "Reckin I sleep practical most of my waking time, so to speak. As fer warshin', well, I never could cotton to tub warshin', being from Tennessee original. Creek warshin' more er less being the style there, ain't never shook it, I reckin." He spoke softly, conversationally. A strange bandido!

The candle weakened. The old man fell asleep, sagging in the chair. Josey Wales lifted his feet, unstrapped the pistol belt from the ranch foreman at his feet and laid it on the table beside Chato. He stepped to the door and studied the heavens.

In a moment, he turned and shook Ten Spot. "Time to relieve Pablo," he said.

The gambler rose, strapped on his pistol and stepped through the door without a word. Pablo came in. He walked to En-lo-e, and kneeling beside her, stroked her hair, listened to her breathing. Then he too stretched on the floor and slept.

In the deepest black of night, there is a breath of wind, different, that tells of the coming birth of dawn, as the rhythmic pangs warn the woman of the coming of her child. Josey Wales knew that breath, back there in Missouri.

He felt it; and rousing from his curious half sleep, he walked to Chato, lying on the table. He shook the vaquero gently. "Chato," he whispered.

"Si, Josey."

"How far ye reckin from here, going north, is thet big deep canyon we come through on the way down?"

Chato shook the sleep from his head. "It will be twenty-five, maybe thirty miles, Josey. Why?"

"Jest figgerin'," the outlaw answered. He walked to the door, and whistled Ten Spot in. Toeing Pablo awake, and then En-lo-e, he said, "We're moving. Git the guns, pack grub, fill grain sacks fer the hosses. Chato, ye lay where ye're at, till we're ready. Ye can have thet white-handled pistol there."

"Gracias, Josey," Chato said, surprised at this uncharacteristic generosity of Josey Wales.

"It's more in the way of a loan," Josey said drily. "Ye got but one pistol. Ye'll be needing two after a while."

They were saddled now, Chato's feet again tied in the stirrups. They took the two horses from the hacienda. En-lo-e sitting astride one, Ten Spot leading the other.

The old man stood in the candlelight of the kitchen door. "So," he said indignantly, "you are horse thieves as well. A hanging offense, I warn you."

From the back of the roan, Josey looked down at the old man. "Jest borrerin' the hosses, so to speak. We ain't leaving no fresh hosses fer Escobedo."

"Escobedo!" the old man exclaimed. "So it is Capitan Jesus Escobedo who pursues you. He is my friend. I warn you, when he arrives, I shall tell him the direction in which you have fled." He stuck out his little chest. "Unless, of course, you murder me now."

"You do thet, old man," drawled Josey, "and if Escobedo is yore friend, watch yer back whilst he's around."

[177]

He clucked the roan into motion, leading Chato's horse; En-lo-e followed, and Pablo. Ten Spot brought up the rear. Into the black before dawn they walked, slowly north. A pitifully slow gait. A long way from the Rio Grande.

16

The wind freshened. It was new from the coming dawn. Later it would grow tired, and mean, and hot.

The single file walked north; the horses' gait, set by Josey in the lead, was a long stride that sometimes caused the shorter-legged horse of En-lo-e to break into a brief trot, but not Chato's.

Gray in the east, and the light daggers shot their arrows into the spaceless sky. Sun broke the rim on their right and made changing colors of the brush, the cactus, the spiny plants. The wind was cold.

The ground elevated gradually. When the sun was an hour high, Josey halted his horse, pulling Chato beside him. The vaquero still slumped in the saddle, but he was conscious. Looking at the bandages, Josey saw fresh blood, only a little, but fresh blood, soaking through. He grunted in disappointment.

Ten Spot came up from the rear, and with him, Pablo and En-lo-e. Ten Spot turned his blistered face backward, then up at the sun. "How you figuring, Josey? The chances?"

Josey plug-cut tobacoo and cheeked it. His jaws worked slowly as he judged the sun. He hooked a lazy leg over his saddle horn, while the horses blew their sides and rested.

"I figger Escobedo is might near a hour on the trail," he said.

"But it will take him time, will it not, to trail you?" Pablo asked.

"Nope. Na'ar bit," Josey said grimly. "Ye all made that ride to the hayceenda in six hour, walking. I made it in four, trotting easy." He chewed some more, frowning at the figgerin'. A horned toad, in the westward shade of a rock, received a dead hit splat on his head and staggered beneath the rock.

"Escobedo—his riders will cut my trail from the arroyo in fifteen minute of fust light. They'll trail fer a while, till they see the tracks heading dead east. Escobedo knows this country. He's 'quainted that water is at the hayceenda. After thet, he won't trail. He'll tail-whup them hosses straight in. I figger three hour fer Escobedo to make the hayceenda."

"Three hours!" The shocking realization made Chato almost shout. "Why, at our gait, Josey, in three hours we will be but halfway to the canyon. He will catch us in an additional three. He will catch us at the canyon. The canyon is a death trap!"

"They's death traps scattered all over creation," Josey drawled. "Good Lord made more briers than He did flowers."

He clucked the roan into motion and led them on. But Chato would not be satisfied. He was alarmed, feverish. "Listen," he called to Josey, "listen to me, you idiota! Lope the horse, ride faster, I can stand it! I swear on my father's head!"

The words of Josey Wales drifted back to him. "Ye ain't got no pa, ye damned bastard, shet up!"

"All right, then," Chato said indignantly, "then let me drift off into the brush. They will not follow one track. I know this country. I can make it. You, then, can easily outrun him for the border. Allow me this honor!"

Chato watched the impassive back of Josey before him. There was no answer; only the back, swaying in the saddle. He cursed Josey Wales, calling him obscenities that would have brought death to other men; he cursed him with the passionate abandonment only a loving brother who had shared the brush of death could do. The impassive back swayed on. Chato spent his strength and slumped forward again.

From behind him, the cool voice of Ten Spot floated to his ears. "After you riding in, after you and Josey coming two hundred miles to pull a worthless saloon bum from a dungeon. Chato, I will shoot you in the back before I will see you ride into the brush."

Pablo wondered at these men, cursing each other. Risking their lives, one for the other, then threatening. And the cold voice of Ten Spot meant what he said, threatening to shoot him in the back. It was a wonderment beyond the comprehension.

The prairie sprouted more rocks. The ground rose steeper. Weakly now, Chato said, "When we go into the canyon, Josey, Escobedo will send riders along the rim. They will shoot us like pigs in a pen. You comprendes, this, of course," he added bitterly.

Josey spat at a side bush. "Reckin he will if'n we don't make it past the fust quarter mile."

"The first quarter mile?" puzzled Chato.

"The fust quarter mile," Josey repeated. " 'Bout a quarter mile in, they's canyons running east and west, seven, maybe ten miles splitting out from the sides of the canyon. They's cliff canyons he cain't jump ner ride into. If he sends his riders around 'em, cost 'em three, maybe four hours."

"I had not noticed, when we came," Chato said.

" 'Taint yore business to notice," Josey drawled. "Ye're a wuthless cow-trailer thet misses half yer rope throws at a steer. Boar coon, coming down the mountains, if'n he don't take notice of the brier patches and trees he might need in a hurry coming back up thet mountain, he's a damn fool boar coon. My pa didn't raise no damn fool boar coons."

By the sun time, Josey figgered three hours. They halted in the climb, while he pulled the long-glass and searched backward. He guessed they had made fifteen miles from the hacienda. From his higher elevation, he swept the prairie below. The glass was not strong enough to bring out the details; but he could reason the lump on the prairie—the hacienda. And coming close, maybe a mile from the east, a huge dust cloud—many horses, coming fast.

He grunted. "Called it might near on the nose," he said with satisfaction. He called to those behind him. "Escobedo is mighty near the hayceenda. Seed his dust." He clucked the roan into motion, but doggedly refused to increase the walking gait.

The old man would tell Escobedo of the badly wounded vaquero, the Apache girl. He would tell Escobedo that the band of Josey Wales could not put up a hard ride. He would tell.

The telling would cost Escobedo thirty minutes, while he blew his horses, watered them. Thirty minutes.

Josey had known the brute foreman was not dead. Propping his boot heels on the belly, he had felt the tensed muscles as the foreman had tried to hide his breathing. From beneath his hat, he had watched; the eyes slit, looking. So he had taken the gun belt. He had taken the two horses—not for the reason he had told the old man. Two horses, fresh, would mean nothing to Escobedo. He'd have to bring his whole crew. But had he left the horses, the foreman would have ridden out to round up the riders of the hacienda and join the chase. The old man would have ridden to intercept Escobedo, and turned him northeast.

Josey had lied to the old man why he took the horses. No sense giving any idears to sich as them. It added a little edge.

The horses were laboring now, the climb steeper, the sun hotter. But the mind of Josey Wales was not on the sun. Valdez would tell Escobedo that he found no dead Josey Wales in Coyamo. Escobedo would guess the arroyo ambush as that of Josey Wales. The old man would confirm it: Josey Wales was alive.

Josey Wales! With a mestizo vaquero, a one-armed, stupid peon! Josey figgered as he rode. Sich would be the outrage of a uppity feller, figgerin' he was better than sich trash, it would might near make him lose his entire sense of reasonableness. Sounded reasonable.

Josey, reading the sign of Escobedo, he was sich a man. And as a few years later the crafty Sitting Bull would figure the thinking of the egotistical Custer, and feed that egotism, and slaughter him, so the mind of Josey Wales worked on the character of the leader chasing him.

Another thought, a small awareness that had rattled

about in his head, began to grow. Everywhere they had been on the trail of Escobedo—the Apache tracks! Always. Now, slitting his eyes with narrow intentness, he watched the side of the trail.

Another hour, and he halted the horses. With the long-glass he looked backward and saw the dust cloud coming north.

"They're coming," he announced laconically, and moved the horses into motion again. Head down, he watched the edge of the trail. Faintly he saw the tracks, but he frowned, puzzled. They were headed away from the trail, southwest. He motioned Pablo forward. "Ask En-lo-e 'bout them tracks." He pointed.

Pablo spoke to the girl. She swung from her horse and knelt in the dirt. She squatted, studying them. She crawled along their path, twenty, thirty yards toward the southwest. Then she rose and came back. She spoke softly to Pablo, and with her hand motioned north.

"She say," Pablo interpreted, "that the tracks point to the southwest, but they are not going that way. Sometime the Apache run backward ten, twenty miles. The earth-deep is on the toe, not the heel. The sand that flip outward is from the toe, forward, not the heel. The Apache —they are men of her band—they are running backward, for the canyon."

The revelation brought a surprised grunt from Josey Wales. The wind was hot, baking the ground red and yellow, loosing its sand on the upward slope. Josey pushed the horses, blowing froth from their bits, heaving their sides. An hour of such riding brought them to the crest, the plateau. Here they halted, and every head turned backward to look. Far down the long, bouldered slope, they could see them. They were strung out in a long line, just beginning the climb from the desert floor.

" 'Pears we're powerful important," Josey drawled, chewing, and watching the troops.

"Looks like the whole army of Mexico," Ten Spot said. "This Escobedo must be crazy."

"Figgers," Josey nodded in satisfaction, "jest half crazy will do."

They rested the horses a quarter hour. Pablo looked nervously at the oncoming riders. They were beginning to mount the slope.

"Let's move," Josey said. He needn't have urged them.

They crowded their horses close behind. Chato had said nothing. Though conscious, he hung his head down, holding to the saddle horn.

It was easier riding across the plateau, a tableland of patched grass, saguaro cactus and stunted mesquite. The horses' stride was easier and stronger.

Though it was still morning, the sun was high when they saw the mouth of the canyon, a shallow cavern at first, teethed with barren rocks. In less than an hour they had entered it, and almost immediately the trail slanted downward, and the walls on either side rose higher.

The path narrowed and beneath the horses' hoofs was almost solid stone, so that sometimes they slipped on the smoothness. Deeper they plunged along the path, always leading down; and when there seemed no end to its descent, it suddenly leveled out. Three hundred feet above them they could see the rim of the plateau.

Josey picked up the stride of the horses, and though none of them spoke their relief, each felt the exultation as they passed the canyons, splitting east and west, of which Josey had spoken.

Deep canyons. Escobedo's riders at least would not be riding the rims above them.

Josey led them on. The mystic vision that was

Geronimo's did not belong to Josey Wales; but their minds were the minds of guerrillas, and so their channels of thought would run alike on the choice of timing, of terrain. So it was, as Josey rode.

He watched the narrowing sides of the canyon. His eyes recognized the place as they rode into it. Scarcely room for two horses to ride abreast; the sides too steep for a horse to climb, rocked and bouldered. Such terrain lasted for perhaps a hundred yards, before the trail widened slightly, the walls gave more slope. Josey led his little band through the hundred yards of narrowed canyon, the horses' hoofs echoing on the hard stone. Any whisper carried in the canyon, and echoed.

At the end of this stretch, Josey halted the horses and dismounted. Pulling his rope from the saddle horn, he tied the reins of all the horses to it, except the roan. He led them into a narrow clump of mesquite, securing them to the bushes.

Chato sagged, held up by Ten Spot and Pablo. En-lo-e watched Josey closely, her eyes unnaturally bright.

Josey chewed and watched the sun almost directly overhead. There was not a breeze in the canyon. High above, the wind, as though playing a flute over the narrow canyon, sounded distant, agonizing a high-pitched note of monotony. They listened. Far away, there was the rapid clatter of horses.

"They're coming, Josey!" Ten Spot exclaimed. Josey spat on a hot rock.

"Nope," he said softly, "them's two hosses. Escobedo sent 'em ahead, see if we made it past the canyons. Listen!"

The horses' hoofs stopped for a moment, then echoed back, going farther and farther away.

"They're going back now," Josey said casually. "Ten Spot, ye climb near to the rim in them rock on the west side, not high 'nough to skyline ye, but high. Pablo, ye and

En-lo-e, ye climb, same wall, twenty feet below Ten Spot. Find ye some good rock to git behint. I'll put Chato a little uppards along the rocks to git his spot. He'll handle the rifle. Give En-lo-e one of them Rurales pistols. Pass out the ammunition. Remember, nobody shoots till I do."

Ten Spot stepped close to Josey. "If we're bushwhacking, Josey, seems to me some of us should be on the eastern wall. Catch them in a cross-fire."

Josey looked patiently at him, as one looks at the unknowing child. "Fust place, they ain't got nowheres to go, nobody kin git up thet wall. Second," he looked at the sun, "minute er two that sun'll be bringing a shade down our western side; they'll be in the sun, looking inter it, our shooting'll come from the shadows. Understand?"

"I would not have thought of it," Ten Spot murmured.

They passed out the guns, the belts, the ammunition; and clambered up the rocks, almost perpendicular. Gently Josey pulled Chato's arm around his neck, and slowly with ginger steps they moved up the wall. Halfway up, he found the rock, and laid Chato behind it.

Beside him he laid the carbine and the cartridge belt. The vaquero lay flat on his stomach, head down toward the canyon. He struggled to his elbows and lifted the carbine.

"She's seven-shot, Chato," Josey said. "I'm depending on ye to shave the ones down around Escobedo so I git to him fust. Remember, Escobedo is mine."

Chato looked up at Josey. "And you, Josey . . ." Tears ran down the face of Chato. "You . . . ," he choked, "you mean to die down there . . . in the canyon."

Josey Wales looked hard on the vaquero. "I ain't never aimed to die nowheres. I aim to kill Escobedo, which I set out as obliged to do in the fust place." His eyes softened, and his voice, as he turned. "Ye'll do, Chato; rec'lect ye're a better man than ye think."

Chato watched, eyes blearing, as Josey picked his way carefully down the wall.

They watched him from the canyon wall. The sun tilted more, and the shadow crossed over Ten Spot. Josey Wales was on the floor of the canyon. He was rubbing down the legs of the roan, picking up his hoofs, removing pebbles. They watched as he slid the big pistols up and down in his holsters; only then did he swing aboard. He didn't move the horse. The roan seemed to know. He stood, still as a rock. Josey swung a leg lazily over the saddle horn and pulled the long knife.

Ten Spot, watching, breathed to himself, "Cutting his tobacco, by heaven!"

Josey did, and chewed slowly, slowly, checking the shadow inch down the western rim, and listening.

Far away, at the beginning, the sound came, like the distant patter of rain. Then closer. Now the clip-clops of the horses sounded plainly, echoing and re-echoing until they filled the canyon with sound. The sound rose from a grumble into a roar. So many horses! deafening! They came in sight. The army officer at their head, saber swinging; behind him in column of twos, the Rurales. On and on they came, an endless stream. A formidable sight.

The shadow had moved farther down the western wall, but Josey Wales, now both feet in the stirrups, sat stolidly in the path, brilliant in the sunlight as it picked the fire-red from the magnificent roan beneath him.

The army officer was fifty yards from Josey before he saw him. The still, stolid horseman had not caught his eyes. He held up his hand in a halt. He peered beneath his cap brim at the figure, sitting like stone.

Josey Wales tied his reins together, hanging them loosely around the saddle horn. He needed no rein control over the roan; Big Red had made too many charges, faced too many such men on horseback. He knew, and his muscles trembled beneath Josey's legs in anticipation.

They sat silently for a long moment. A whispering line of sound ran back down the ranks of Rurales. Suddenly the shout came; it was filled with rage, mad as a mad-man, and it came from the throat of Josey Wales. "ESCOBEDO!" And it echoed, "ESCOBEDO! ESCObedo! Escobedo! escobedo!" Far down the canyon, the echo carried the name and the rage.

The army officer pulled a saber and raised it, glinting in the sun. "I am Capitan Jesus Escobedo!" "JESUS Escobedo! jesus escobedo!"—the echo carried the tone of arrogance with it.

The echo died, and for a full minute there was silence, and the voice came flat, hard, taunting, snarling: "I be JOSEY WALES!" "JOSEY Wales! josey wales!" The echo rang away, and a quiver of motion ran the rank of Rurales; the whispering of their voices echoed also, "Josey Wales!"

When Josey shouted again, the voice was not loud, but flat and murderously vicious. "Git something in yer hand, ye yeller-livered slime. I'm going to kill ye!" And the echo carried "kill ye . . . kill ye . . ."

Lieutenant Valdez moved his horse to come beside his Capitan. Chato wiped the sweat from his eyes. He didn't even use a chest shot; he was that good. He blew the side of Valdez' head off. The Lieutenant toppled from the saddle. The crack of the rifle sent ominous sounds through the Rurales. They slid rifles from their scabbards.

The Sergeant moved his horse forward, and the rifle cracked again, knocking him, almost headless, to the ground.

Escobedo sat alone. "You will face him alone!" Chato panted beneath his breath, "you will face him alone . . . as long as I live."

FORREST CARTER

Escobedo dropped the saber. His face was white, either crazed or frightened. He reached and pulled the rifle from its scabbard.

As he did, Josey Wales leaned forward. "GIT, RED!"

The roan leaped in a half rear, front feet coming off the ground. The horse before him was his enemy, he knew from so many times before. The .44's were in both hands of Josey Wales.

Escobedo was slow with the rifle, he sunk spurs to his horse, but he had already lost the edge.

The roan was in a dead run. Josey raised the pistols. One boomed like cannon from the walls of the canyon, then the other. Escobedo flipped backward from his horse, his chest blown out. Still the roan plunged, knocking the horse of Escobedo sprawling in the trail.

Josey whirled him with his knees in a rearing turn and with deliberate methodical action fired into the body on the ground; once, twice, three times. He paid no attention to the line of Rurales so close. He spat on Capitan Jesus Escobedo.

The Rurales were frozen in this instant of brutal action; now they charged. If they expected the lone horseman to flee, they were badly surprised. With his knees, he whirled the roan to face them, and charged into them hammering the pistols, booming from his hands.

From the western wall the rifle cracked, again and again. The pistols began to fire from the rocks. And out of it all, began—low, then rising higher, higher into a scream of inhuman exultation—the blood-fight lusting yell of the rebel, Josey Wales. It tingled the spine of Chato. Pablo shivered at the sound. The Rurales ceased their shouting curses. The scream broke, echoing down the canyon over and over.

Ten Spot was no gunfighter. There was really no violence in Ten Spot, the derringer he had carried was a pretense.

[190]

He had gambled, but before that, it had been his apple trees and his books.

And so from his books, the gallant picture of the six-teenth-century duelists was all he knew. He rose, standing erect; one hand on hip, he raised the pistol and cocked; with deliberate aim he fired, knocking a Rurale from the saddle. His ruffled shirt fluttered in the wind. The fine black frock coat gave him the picture of himself in his mind. Again, he raised the pistol. He was no longer Ten Spot. He was William Francis Beauregard Willingham.

Rurales spotting the tall figure raised their rifles and fired. Two of them hit, knocking Ten Spot down. It was undignified. He struggled back to his feet, weaving, blood running from his chest. He deliberated his aim, careful to place his left hand on his hip. Five rifle slugs riddled his body. His gun, already cocked, fired. He stood, swaying, and plunged stiffly through the air, like the statue of a statesman toppled by vandals. He plunged, turning in the air, and smashed against the rocks at the bottom. At last. William Francis Beauregard Willingham was dead.

The Rurales, finding only two abreast could charge the madman, feeling the killing fire from the wall, turned to run. As they did, the figures came out of the rocks on either side. APACHE!

With bows and arrows, lances and guns, they fell on the Rurales. The first horseman to escape was galloping head-long, when the squat figure leaped behind him on the horse and split open his skull like a melon with a hatchet. The powerful Apache then whirled the horse, and with lance leveled, raced back down the path. If the scar-faced would plug the neck of the bottle, Geronimo would hold the bottom!

The screams of dying men were cut short by the sog-ging sound of the lances striking home. Wounded horses whickered and tried to rise. The Apache moved among them. Where they found men with the scalps of their women, their children, they butchered their bodies.

Josey Wales had dismounted. Sweat covered the blood running from his side, the saber slash on his shoulder.

Slowly he walked to the battered body of Ten Spot, lying almost in the trail. Pablo and En-lo-e stumbled down the rocks, supporting Chato between them. They stood in a little circle, exhausted, and looked at Ten Spot. His body was broken, bloodied beyond recognition.

Tiredly Josey Wales bent and began to remove the rocks, deep enough and long enough to bury Ten Spot among them. He moved slowly, rolling the body into the hole. Chato stood, swaying, while Pablo and En-lo-e helped pile the rocks, making the mound. They paid no attention to the Apache warriors fifty yards up the canyon, stripping the bodies of guns, ammunition, rounding up the horses. Now the trail was in shadow.

Josey pulled his hat from his head. His face looked vacant. Pablo and Chato pulled their sombreros, holding them over their breasts.

"Well," Josey said, and his voice was hollow, "reckin we got to say something."

"Si," Pablo said, "we must give Señor Ten Spot the burial."

"Lord . . . ," Josey began.

"Si," Pablo said.

"Shet up!" Josey snarled, "cain't ye see I'm a-prayin'? Lord," he began again, "Ten Spot wa'ant his name, but I cain't rec'lect off-hand what it was. It was a long un, and Ye'll know it, I reckin." Josey paused and frowned. "Ten Spot never meant nothing by stacking a deck, er bottom-sliding a card. It was jest didn't mean thet much to him. He obliged me, Lord, as I come to pay thet obligation. Reckin he died without a speck o' yeller. We'd 'preciate Ye considering Ten Spot." Josey paused again. "Ashes to ashes, dust to dust, Lord gives and takes away—and sich. Amen!" He placed his hat on his head.

"Amen!" said Chato. "Adios, Ten Spot."

"Amen," Pablo said, and crossed himself. He had not known prayers were said in such a manner.

"Does he not—Señor Ten Spot," Pablo asked quietly, "does he not need something to mark his grave?"

Josey cut a tobacco plug and chewed on the question for a long minute. "Noooooo," he said, "I rec'lect Rose telling me oncet thet Ten Spot when he was drunk talked continual about a place called Shenandoah, a valley which was green, and about some apple trees of his'n." He paused. "No, I reckin that's where Ten Spot's gone, not here. Could be," and the scarred face brightened, "could be he's taken Rose along with him. No," he seemed satisfied, "Ten Spot ain't here."

Pablo and Josey, supporting the stumbling Chato between them, walked to where the horses were tied, and mounted. Josey leading Chato, Pablo following. En-lo-e hesitated. She looked back. The Apache were standing, silent, watching. She waved, and leaped astride the horse, following Pablo down the shadowed trail.

The Apache returned to their work, hanging the guns and ammunition across the horses, stringing the extra horses together, the captured prizes of war. "Loot" the white man would call it—unless he took it himself.

They rode in a long line, Geronimo at their head, down the same trail taken by Josey Wales. They passed the grave of Ten Spot. They did not stop or look at the small bandaged Apache standing by the mound.

It was unbecoming to display emotion. Anything felt by the Apache could be, and was, translated into action; but sometimes, sorrow—there was no way. And so they did not look, for they would not embarrass their brother Na-ko-la.

Na-ko-la stood by the grave as the shadows lengthened.

He squatted, and sang the death song for the hero, which sounds as a savage, meaningless chant to the ear of the white man, but he sang:

"You have helped the helpless who could not help you
You have befriended the friendless who could not be your
*   friend*
You have died the death of bravery and courage
You will come back in the great circle
You will be born again, Brother, higher in the great
*   circle, for your deeds have earned you this place*
I, Na-ko-la, have sung, so the spirits of the circle of life
*   will hear my humble song for you."*

Na-ko-la stood. The song was finished. Tears came into his eyes. The Apache feels deeply. Na-ko-la cried. He stumbled away down the trail. Turning, he called back, "Adios, Sonofabitch!"

Fifty yards down the trail, he found the horse tied to a bush, left for him by his comrades. He mounted and followed their tracks. They would wait.

17

Far down the trail, the canyon wall sloped gently upward
to the plateau. It was here that Josey led them, until they
came again to the plains.

The sun was low and firing the prairie with a crimson
haze, scattering the red paint of dust in the air and on the
cactus and the brush. They continued north over a slight
roll and felt the cooling breath of the evening come,
spreading the death shroud on the day.

Pablo eased his horse beside Chato. "Chato, what good
has come of it all? The killing—Señor Ten Spot is dead."

Chato shrugged his shoulders. "Must good come of it,
niño? It was the obligation. It is paid." Chato softened his
voice. "Perhaps good comes sometimes. Quien sabe? Who

know? Maybe the wiping out of Escobedo's Rurales will bring El Presidente Juarez north to investigate. I comprendes he love his people and travel about in a plain carriage and will not have even one guardia. Maybe," Chato shrugged again, "the zapotas, the buzzard politicos who fly around him, will confuse him. Quien sabe?" Then Chato said quietly, "Josey?"

"Yeah?"

"Look, back there behind us."

Josey stopped the horses. Lined up on the knoll over which they had come were the Apache. They sat their horses silently and did not move. They were watching Josey Wales, and his little band. Below the knoll, halfway between the Apache and Josey Wales, a mule was tied to a bush. On its back were heavy sacks, sacks loaded with something.

En-lo-e broke her horse into a run, riding to the knoll. She talked with the squat, powerful leader who sat his horse in the center of the line. Now she came back, but only as far as the mule. She motioned to Pablo. Pablo rode to meet her. He dismounted and he and En-lo-e talked, and talked.

Josey crooked a leg around his saddle horn and pushed his hat back from the hard face. "Shore hope we ain't got to tussle them none. I'm mighty near tuckered out."

"I too," Chato said, "am heavily tuckered."

Pablo rode back. He got down from the horse. He still wore the sandals and ragged pants of the peon. He stood and looked at the ground and finally up at Josey.

"She say," Pablo began hesitantly, "she say there is a valley high in the Mother Mountains where the soldado cannot come, where the político cannot reach. She say there is a stream of water that . . ." Pablo paused. "The sacks have kernels of maize, bigger than the thumb,

Josey," his voice rose in excitement, "and the bean, the squash, she say . . ."

"I know what she say," Josey said tiredly.

Pablo hung his head. He looked up at Josey with the humble yet stubborn will that Josey Wales first recognized in him. He took Josey's hand in his own. "I am sorry, Josey. I cannot be a vaquero, a bandido. I—I cannot."

"What," Josey Wales asked sternly, "makes ye think I give a damn what ye are?" But then, with the closest emotion to kindliness that could touch the eyes of Josey Wales, he said softly, "Don't be sorry, son, take your woman to the valley. Raise yore corn, feel good in the honest sweat, lay by the side of yore woman in the evening without listening fer a foot er a hoss. Sleep the good sleep. Be happy, Pablo!"

If there was sadness in the voice of Josey Wales— perhaps there was—then it was of a little mountain farm far away, and too long ago, for the man, now made, to go back.

Tears filled the eyes of Pablo. He shook Chato's hand, and gave the reins of his horse to the vaquero. He walked to the mule. He helped En-lo-e astride the mule. He climbed aboard her horse. He felt he must say something in farewell, and so he waved the stump of his arm. "The first niño," he shouted, "will be name Chato Josey!"

Chato laughed and shouted, "Gracias!"

"Go to hell," said Josey Wales. Pablo grinned, for he knew. Josey Wales only rarely would say the words he felt. He rode, leading the mule and En-lo-e, and the sacks of corn.

Ahead of him the Apache turned their horses toward the mountain, guiding him to the Mother. Only one remained on the knoll. He watched the retreating Chato and the scar-face fading to the north for a long time.

[197]

He would fight, nearly twenty years more. He would strike and run and strike again. In one year, with only nineteen warriors, and with Mexican soldados harassing his flanks and his rear, he would fight a United States general with five thousand troops, he would fight him to a standstill. During that time, he would lose only one warrior.

If it is so, as the militarists say, that guerrilla warfare is a warfare of the mind, then the most brilliant mind in the history of guerrilla action must belong to Geronimo. But history would record him as the murderous renegade. He cared nothing for the written pages of the white men. Pages of paper mold and rot and wither away.

Only the spirit grows and lives—lives forever.

Geronimo turned his horse and followed the warriors, and En-lo-e and Pablo.

But first, like Josey Wales, he scanned the horizon, noted the wind that waved the bush, listened to the sounds and read the track in the sand.

18

They rode far into the night toward the Rio Grande, as far as Josey dared, until Chato swayed so violently in the saddle, his horse stumbled. Only then did Josey pull off into thick brush. He pulled Chato from his horse. From the canteens, he poured water into his hat and watered the horses and fixed nose bags of grain to their bridles.

Pulling Chato's saddle to him, he laid the vaquero's head on it and covered him with a blanket against the cold wind. Only then did he open his shirt and inspect the ugly bullet gash along his own side. He stripped a shirt and bound himself tightly. Pulling down the fringed jacket, he checked the slash of the saber. It was not deep, and using his teeth, he knotted another bandage around it.

Chato was awake as he finished. "Es malo? Is it bad, Josey?"

"It ain't bad," Josey said quietly.

Digging a shallow hole, he set a fire, where he suspended the can of water and jerky beef to boil.

Chato reached into his saddlebag and brought forth the bottle of tequila. He held it aloft. "Mine!" he announced proudly, "and is all full." He pulled the cork and swallowed long. Wiping his mouth with the back of his hand, he said, "I will say this, Josey, for Señor Escobedo, he keep the best tequila everywhere I have tasted it." To verify this truth, he took a long pull from the bottle again.

Josey watched the fire. "Go ahaid," he drawled, "git drunk. Ye'll make good bait by the fire fer any passing throat-cutter, whilst I sleep in the bresh."

Chato was feeling the warmth of the tequila. "You know, Josey," he said philosophically, "if it was, that I was not Chato Olivares, you know who I would want to be?"

"Let me guess," Josey said drily, poking at the tiny flame. "Ye'd want to run a whorehouse in San Antone?"

Chato took no offense. He smiled. Drunkenly, but carefully, he corked the bottle and laid it by his side with a comforting pat. "No, Josey," he said dreamily, "if it was that I was not Chato Olivares, I would want to be Pablo." He closed his eyes, smiling, and slept.

Josey pulled the can from the flames and wolfed down the stew. Pulling his saddle and blanket into the darkness of the brush, he lay down, rolling the blanket around him against the wind; but first, he laid the .44 across his belly.

Chato lay, as he had been promised, near the fire.

They were up before dawn, Josey pouring stew down Chato and tying his feet in his stirrups. Sun broke the eastern rim as they splashed their horses across the Rio Grande at Santo Rio. The town was asleep.

They did not ride the street, but crossed behind the Lost Lady Saloon, behind the hotel, near the barn where Pablo had hid. Josey stopped the horses at the side of the three square boards, already bent and weathering. The lettering on each was simple: MELINA—KILLED 1868; KELLY—KILLED 1868; ROSE—KILLED 1868. As sparse perhaps as their lives had been.

Josey pulled their horses close to the graves. The wind was cold, and the roan sidestepped against it. He pulled his hat lower against the blowing dust, and from his pocket he pulled an object and dropped it on the grave of Rose. It was the glass earring. The wind rolled it, pushing it against the board, and sand began to cover its glitter.

"It's done, Rose," Josey said quietly. The roan stomped and sidled. He turned him into the wind.

"Si," Chato said, as he passed the leaning board, "it is done."

They rode northwest, quartering the horses into a blue norther wind. They did not stop at noon; and late, as the sun touched the jagged teeth of the buttes to the west, they saw the Crooked River mountains.

A line of horsemen were to the west, silhouetted against the sun high on a ridge. "Comanch," Josey said. He pulled the long-glass and watched. A huge fat cloud of smoke rose in the air, followed by a smaller cloud, and then a third that was waved toward Crooked River.

Josey swung the long-glass to the mountains of the ranch. A thin ash smoke rose, followed by another, another and another. It was the thin smoke of the Cherokee.

"Well," he grinned at Chato, "Comanch sent the word. Big cloud, big chief, meaning me—little cloud, which means a hombre wuth next to nuthin', thet's you— waving it north, means we're coming in. T'other smoke," he added with a satisfied air, "that was Lone, thanking 'em fer the message."

Chato raised his bottle of tequila. The wound was hurting. "To hell with it," he said, referring to the little cloud.

Dusk had fallen when they rounded the mountain, into the warmth and the grass of Crooked River Ranch. "By God," Josey said, "even from here I kin smell Granma's cooking. She'll have a big un fixed up fer us." He quickened the gait of the horses, who were bending, snatching at the long grass, as they walked.

"Josey," Chato said.

"Yeah?"

"You will not tell Granma of the puta and me in Saucillo, eh?" They rode on, and Josey Wales made no answer.

"Josey?"

"Yeah, I heerd ye," Josey said.

"You know the belt I·have, the one with silver concho for a buckle. You have always wanted it. Once you tried to trade with mc, eh? If you will not tell Granma of the puta, the belt is yours. What you say, Josey?" Chato's voice was anxious.

They rode further in silence. Josey was chewing and considering. A longhorn snorted and trotted away. After a long time, the words floated back to Chato. "I reckin," said Josey.

The soul of Chato Olivares was now at peace. Granma would keep him resting, maybe even a month, while he sat beneath the big cottonwood and watched the others work. The belt, it was nada. He could always borrow ahead on the wages for another. Peace—for even the Comanche knew: the word of Josey Wales was true.